WINTER IN MONTREAL

Picas Series 11

Canadä

Guernica Editions Inc. acknowledges the support of
The Canada Council for the Arts.
Guernica Editions Inc. acknowledges the support of
the Ontario Arts Council.
Guernica Editions Inc. acknowledges the financial support of the
Government of Canada through the Book Publishing Industry
Development Program (BPIDP).
This publication was assisted by the Minister of Foreign Affairs
(Government of Italy) through the Istituto Italiano di Cultura in
Toronto (Carlo Coen: Director).

PIETRO CORSI

WINTER IN MONTREAL

TRANSLATION BY ANTONIO DI GIACOMANTONIO

GUERNICA
TORONTO·BUFFALO·LANCASTER (U.K.)
2000

Original title in Italian: *La Giobba*
Published in 1982 by Edizioni Enne, Campobasso, Molise (ly)
Copyright © 2000, by Pietro Corsi and Guernica Editions .
Translation © 2000, by Antonio di Giamantonio
and Guernica Editions Inc.
Preface Copyright © 2000, by Sante Matteo.
Afterword Copyright © 2000, by Giose Rimanelli.

Antonio D'Alfonso, editor
Guernica Editions Inc.
P.O. Box 117, Station P, Toronto (ON), Canada M5S 2S6
2250 Military Road, Tonawanda, N.Y. 14150-6000 U.S.A.
Gazelle, Falcon House, Queen Square, Lancaster LA1 1RN U.K.
Tyepset by Selina.
Printed in Canada.

Legal Deposit – Third Quarter
National Library of Canada
Library of Congress Catalog Card Number: 00-107505
Canadian Cataloguing in Publication Data
Corsi, Pietro
[Giobba. English]
Winter in Montreal
(Picas series ; 11)
Translation of: La giobba.
ISBN 1-55071-117-2
I. Di Giacomantonio, Antonio. II. Title.
III. Title: Giobba. English. IV. Series.
PS8555.o6674G5613 2000 C00-901274-5
PR9199.3.C655G5613 2000

CONTENTS

Preface

Pietro Corsi's novel, *Winter in Montreal* seems to be the product of a process of distillation and compression yielding a narrative jewel: small, hard, crystalline. The author has tackled one of the most complex and traumatic of human experiences, that of emi/immigration, and has reduced it to its essential and most revealing elements, stripping away unnecessary accretions to leave behind a translucent story which, in its stark simplicity, is both a touching document of a particular place and time and situation as well as a timeless parable of universal significance. He has accomplished this without reducing his characters and situations to lifeless abstractions or facile stereotypes, and has succeeded in expressing the crucial psychological, social, and anthropological issues which are most immediately and dramatically inherent in the emi/immigrant's experience, but which are ultimately also the basic elements of the human condition in general.

Immigrant narratives such as Corsi's serve as magnifying lenses which allow us to scrutinize the process of humanization, the makeup of human identity. By uprooting individuals from their native environment and placing them in a foreign context, and thus isolating them from many of the "humanizing" elements which previously defined them, writer and readers can better perceive how those humanizing elements function and why they are important.

In many cases, as in the case of Onofrio Annibalini, what we witness is an inexorable process of "dehumanization" as the individual who loses a sense of place and social standing ends up losing a sense of self as well. But, by perceiving and understanding how and why he is "dehumanized" we also come to have a better realization of what "humanity" is, how it is constructed and how it can be destroyed. By witnessing how our humanity can be destroyed we can possibly also come to comprehend how it can be reconstructed and perhaps to realize that it must be reconstructed and redefined constantly.

Pietro Corsi's fellow emigrant from the small hill town of Casacalenda in the Molise region of Southern Italy, novelist and poet Giose Rimanelli, points out that writing, especially for an emigrant writer, is primarily remembering, and thus a way of recuperating and preserving that which would otherwise be lost. It is precisely the stories of the illiterate, disenfranchised, and essentially voiceless Onofrio Annibalinis of the world which are liable to be lost or never recorded. The desperate struggle of a poor, inconsequential individual to find a menial job and make a living in a foreign land is not particularly newsworthy. It is easy to forget or to ignore. Yet it is the most basic and most important struggle of all, all the more significant for its very ordinariness.

The remembering that is writing serves not only the writer, but the readers as well. Through published writing society as a whole remembers and passes its memories to subsequent generations in order to permit a dialogue between ancestors and descendants and to maintain lines of communication between past, present, and future. Historical memory has become both more difficult and more crucial in our modern consumerist societies which induce historical and cultural amnesia in order to foster the ethos of instant gratification which fuels the engine of capitalist production. We are becoming amnesiacs despite, or precisely because of, the proliferation of information and media. The more books, movies, and television shows demand our attention each year the less time we have to retrieve those from the past. The present media overload which caters to immediate consumption impoverishes us by depriving us of our past and atrophies our capacity to project and construct our future.

Why is it important for those of us who are sons and daughters of the Onofrio Annibalinis to remember what it was like for our parents? Because in their stories lie the basic lessons of what it means to live as human beings. This apparently simple account of a poor *contadino*'s (peasant's) futile struggle to make a better life for himself in a new world is indeed valuable as a socio-historical document which informs future generations of what conditions were like in parts of Italy and of Canada after the Second World War. More importantly, however, it is a reminder to all of us, immigrants or not, of the problems and stakes we all face when we try to "make a life" for ourselves.

If writing such as Corsi's is remembering, it is so in two senses: as the opposite of forgetting and as the opposite of dismembering. In the latter sense to "remember" would mean to re-articulate and recompose that which has been taken apart, such as the life of the immigrant Onofrio Annibalini who gave up his identity in his timeless agricultural society and must construct a new identity in a strange new world of constant flux. Having lost his personal and social roots, he must now find some new certitudes which will anchor him in the rushing flow of new, inexplicable situations and experiences, so that he can orient himself, take a bearing, chart a course, and again navigate the river of time/life.

It is not only the immigrant who faces such problems. We all do. We are all emigrants from the past and immigrants in a constantly changing world. Our social context, which is to say our world, is changing all the time and with it our identities as well. Immigrant experiences, such as that remembered in this story of Onofrio Annibalini, crystallize what is otherwise a more gradual and less visible process in all our lives, thus allowing us to perceive it and understand ourselves and our world better.

Sante Matteo
Oxford, Ohio, March 1996

WINTER IN MONTEAL

PART ONE

1

The day before leaving for Canada, Onofrio Annibalini went to visit his friend Michele Scardocchia at his farm-house on the Costa del Lago. He wanted him to be his proxy.

"A man who goes to America needs a proxy," he told himself, "especially if he is leaving property behind."

It was a blistering mid-August day and Onofrio Annibalini was walking with his usual brisk pace along the muletrack that goes from Provvidenti to the Costa del Lago. Now and then he stopped in the shade along the side of the track to wipe the pouring sweat off his brow and rest awhile. In his heart he once again cursed "this filthy town" where he was born and blessed "the dear *compare* Pasquale Petrilli" who had gotten him a work contract in a Canadian factory that enabled him to emigrate.

"This," he said to himself, "this for sure is the last time that these muletracks see me around. I am tired of scratching this earth only for a piece of bread and taxes. I'll go work in America! There, there is such a thing as a pay envelope with dollars in it every week of the month, every month of the year. You can eat all you want, and still have enough money left for a saving at the bank. And when you get old, you can go back home with an American pension and live like a king, smoking cigars on the church steps or at the Fontana della Libera. Nice indeed to put your feet up and enjoy life."

"How is America, zi' Onofrio?" he could hear the youngsters ask, admiringly.

"Eh, America! A blessed land. That's what America is: a blessed land!"

"And the money, how is the money there?"

"The money? They don't call it *lire*, over there. They call it dollar and one only – which you can find even on the ground as you walk about – is worth more than six hundred *lire*."

"And what language do they speak in America?"

"Here we speak Italian, since we are in Italy. There they speak American, no?"

"And how does one manage to work, if one doesn't speak American?"

"All you need to do is work, you don't have to speak. They make you understand to do this, you do it. Then they make you understand to do that, and you do that too. It's that easy, and a lot better than tilling hard and stingy soil."

"And is it easy to find work in America?"

"They have enough work for all of Italy, they have! And if one learns the language, which is the American language as I was saying, then he can even become, say, a surveyor like don Nicola Ardente here, or a notary, like that shoemaker from Casacalenda who went to America when he was twenty years old."

He was now walking ever faster, sweating ever more. Horse-flies buzzed all around him, some landing on his face to suck his sweat while he flailed his hands about his head to chase them away.

As he approached Scardocchia's farm, a barking German shepherd rushed to confront him. After smelling him out the dog stopped barking and started jumping around him, wagging his tail.

"Hey, Miche' . . ." Onofrio yelled out, when he didn't see his friend.

Soon after, a wise-looking old man, nearly bald and rather bent on his back, emerged from the shade behind the farmhouse and came forward to greet him.

"Hey there, Onofrio. What brings you here today?" he asked, fanning himself with an open book.

Michele Scardocchia was considered to be a highly educated farmer. He kept up on things, read books and newspapers, and had been elected Secretary of the Regional Farmer's Union. He was a very competent person and everyone went to him for favors and advice. All in town seemed to agree that he was so well educated as to have acquired even that certain honesty that poor folks could never have, no matter how clever and daring, locked as they were in their perpetual struggle against government bureaucrats and those who know more than them. With the air of someone who was good and unassuming, sometimes allowing himself to be asked and begged, Michele Scardocchia always did his very best to be of service.

"Aren't you leaving tomorrow for the Americas?" Michele Scardocchia asked, when he got close to him.

"Yes, I leave tomorrow and the bus is coming tonight. But, you see, I had forgotten something important . . ."

"Yes, I know. You forgot to say good-bye to an old friend, didn't you?"

"Not just that but also, you see . . ."

Onofrio wanted to say more, but could not muster the courage to continue. He knew that if Scardocchia was not approached in just the right way, you wouldn't get the time of day out of him.

"How can I possibly understand," Scardocchia said impatiently, "if you don't explain?"

"Well, it's just that . . ." Annibalini muttered, unable to express himself even with simple words. "You are a very educated man and . . ."

"Yeees?" remarked Scardocchia, who was beginning to understand that his old pal Annibalini had come to him for a favor. "Go on, go on."

"As I was saying, you are a very educated person, and if we cannot turn to you for a favor, who can we turn to?"

"This is true," Michele Scardocchia admitted, with an air of self-importance.

"Can we go to the Mayor, who doesn't care about us? Or to the priest, who is a doddering old man?"

"You have a point there," his friend agreed, consoling. "You are right and I, honestly, cannot find any fault in your reasoning."

"Thanks. I knew you would understand. You are a true friend of us poor *cafoni*."

"Oh, come on now, Onofrio!" Scardocchia beamed. "I am only a poor farmer myself, remember? And besides, I am not what you all make me out to be. I too am a nobody when it comes to those who look upon us from up high, or from behind a desk."

"Absolutely not!" Onofrio protested, as if personally offended. "It isn't true. When you feel like it, you very well know how to command respect and make yourself heard."

"Well, in a way," Scardocchia shrugged dismissively.

"So I figured, if anyone should have my power of attorney, it's you!"

"Not at all!" Scardocchia sneered. "You are leaving your wife here. Certainly, she can represent you better than I ever could. If I may say so, Onofrio, I really think that she should be your proxy."

"Absolutely not! Let's leave my wife out of this. These are matters of the head, not for women."

"No, I cannot accept," Scardocchia insisted. "Your wife has her rights and, in this matter, she is the only one that counts."

"Let's not talk about her," Annibalini said, lowering his head as if out of shame. "Not after what has happened. You do understand, don't you?"

"Well," Scardocchia said, resigned. "If that's how you look at it, I cannot say no."

"Very well then," Annibalini said thankfully and sincerely moved. "Now you are talking like a gentleman and a true friend."

Michele Scardocchia went inside and put his blue suit on, the same one he had worn the day he got married. He turned the hem of his pants up to protect them from dust, then put his dress shoes in an old but elegant leather briefcase. He carefully folded his jacket and hung it on his arm. He closed the door of the farm-building with padlocks and, together with Annibalini, started out for Casacalenda to see don Domenico Lalli, the Notary who had to draw up the power of attorney.

"What about you, Michele?" Annibalini asked his friend. "Will you ever come to America some day?"

"No. Never!" Michele Scardocchia answered quickly. "I have never even thought about getting away from here. I love this little town of ours so much, that even if I should lack bread to eat, someday, reading and looking

at these surroundings that saw me come into this world,
will be nourishment enough for me."

"This is true," Annibalini agreed, while thinking that
his friend must be a bit of a fool after all. "You are
different, not like the rest of us and better off for it."

"Even so, my friend, it is also true that he who knows
how to make the best out of what he has, enjoys life better
than others," asserted Michele Scardocchia. Then he
added: "And besides, after my wife's death . . ."

Onofrio Annibalini did not speak any more. He withdrew into respectful silence at the memory of the saintly
woman who had been crushed by a speeding car in the
darkness of night, as she was returning home balancing
a bundle of firewood on her head.

They arrived at the outskirts of town. Scardocchia
unfolded his jacket and put it on. He knotted his multicolored bow-tie on his white shirt, took off his heavy
boots and put on his black dress shoes. Lastly, he straightened out the hem of his pants and gently smoothed out
the creases with his hands.

Annibalini had been watching him with a mixture of
envy and slight resentment. He felt that all that meticu-
lousness was out of place in farmers like them. But then
again, he thought, Michele was not just any other farmer.

It took quite a long time to secure the power of
attorney. The Notary, don Domenico Lalli, was not in his
office and they had to wait for him to show up. When he
finally did, since Annibalini was illiterate they had to find
two witnesses to validate his signature, the "X" sign as
for illiterate people.

It was well into the afternoon by the time they got
back to Provvidenti. At the Annibalini residence there
were a lot of people waiting and many more came later.
Some brought salami and some letters; others brought
braids of onions or garlic and others a gold trinket or a

wheel of pecorino cheese: all destined for family and friends in Montreal. There was enough of the stuff to fill up a suitcase or two.

With the arrival of each well-wisher with a packet in hand, Onofrio became gloomy but tried not to show it. He greeted all of them cordially, and there were sweets and pastries with lots of wine for everybody.

In due course the bus arrived and all crates and suitcases were loaded aboard. A quick good-bye to friends and family, and Onofrio Annibalini barely had enough time to remind his new proxy to take good care of his wife, his daughter and his property.

Then off and away. The first step towards that American soil that had been discovered by a Genoese sailor named Giovanni Caboto, as Scardocchia had explained while walking back from Casacalenda.

2

As soon as he finished climbing the stairs at Queen Elizabeth Station in Montreal, Onofrio Annibalini found himself surrounded by a crowd of people from his hometown. His heart, rough and unrefined as only the heart of a rough and unrefined southern farmer can be, a heart that idles and never says anything, not even when sick, that same hardened heart was now utterly moved. His friends took turns kissing him on the cheeks and hugging him, some slapping him heartily on the back while others, shouting familiar greetings, shook hands with him.

He felt as if he were in another world, so very strange yet pleasant. In fact, so strange and pleasant that he felt a rush run through his tear ducts, something like a stream of bile that wanted to flush out. Everything was so different! He could see it in the look of those people who he had not expected to be there waiting for him, and he could feel it all around him. He could see it everywhere: in the posters hanging on walls, in the jackets of the baggage handlers, in the brooms of the floor sweepers.

When they got to the Petrilli's house, and he was alone with the *compare*, his wife Michelina and their two sons, he could hardly remember anything any more. Except, that is, the noise that the locks of the trunks made while popping open, and the confused din of shouting voices.

"It's mine!"

"This is for me!"

"My wife sent me this, you like it?"

"My dear *compare*, come see us sometime, you hear?"

"Just a minute, there. You made a mistake. That one is mine!"

"Good night, everyone!"

While *comare* Michelina was preparing something to eat, all four men gathered in a room where there was a television set every bit as large as a steamship trunk and some small and large couches in which you sank until your knees reached your chin. And there were rugs on the floor, on which he was afraid to step.

At six the following morning, everyone was up and awake, and one by one they all found their way to the kitchen. While the *comare* was busy preparing breakfast, steaming coffee was already waiting on the table.

"Sit down, have a cup of coffee," his *compare* said.

Onofrio began to sip his hot coffee slowly. The few words he was about to say to make small talk got stuck in his throat for his *compare*, or so it seemed to him, had gotten up on the wrong side of the bed.

"Well, *compare*," Petrilli went on, his sullen face glued to the cup. "Dominique and I are going to work. We cannot miss a single day of work here, you see. In this country you go to work even if the wife dies, 'cause if you don't you get fired and finding another job is not easy. Jacques, here, will stay with you. He has been out of work for over a month now, so you both can pack your lunch and start walking these nice long and broad avenues to look for work."

"You mean," Onofrio said, "I'm not going to work in that factory that gave me the work contract?"

"Hell," the *compare* sighed, "the work contract! Everyone knows that work contracts are granted only to allow you to come over. Once here, if you want a job you have to go look for it."

"But we paid for that contract, didn't we? You wrote me to say that you had to pay five hundred dollars."

The *compare* did not answer. He dunked his bread in the coffee and continued eating, his head bent down on the cup. While putting the bread away, his wife sighed and turned to look at Onofrio.

"We sure did," she said, with a shrug of her shoulders. "Five hundred dollars, we paid. But we also wrote to tell you that the factory would give you a job only if one was available at your arrival. Work is difficult to find nowadays. Or didn't my husband just say that poor Jacques, here, has been out of work for two months?"

"I understand, *comare*, I understand," Onofrio said, apologetically. "Small matter, don't get upset. If things are as you say, the *comparello* and I will start walking the streets together and one of these days both of us will find a job. Isn't that so, *comparello?*"

"Sure! I have been looking all this time for a job and have not found one. But now that you are here, *compare*," the young man said sarcastically, "now that you are here it becomes all very easy to find work. We go out together, they see us and they say eh, finally a stout old man has arrived from Italy. A solid and strong man, look here. Of course. And they will take us on right away, *compare*. Do you prefer light or heavy work? And how much would you like to make? That's what they will say, *compare*. Because you're here now . . ."

"Jacques!" his mother yelled out, with a look on her face that could strike a bull dead.

A moment of silence and embarrassment followed. A moment needed to reestablish balance and put things back in perspective.

"Every morning," the other young man said, "Jacques comes out with us, box lunch in hand, and goes around looking for a job. Nothing, *compare*. Nothing! At the factory where I work they promised me that they would take him, but . . ."

" . . . but two days later you were laid off too," the *comare* said bitterly. "Sheer luck that our parish priest, bless his soul, went to talk with the boss and managed to make him understand our predicament. We paid a hundred and fifty dollars and they took him back," she added, talking to Onofrio. "That's how things are now, *compare*. That's how things are nowadays for everyone. Just yesterday our next door neighbor, a woman from Marche, was telling me that where her husband works, a factory that employs over fifteen hundred workers, they've laid off three hundred men. Poor people! I feel so sorry for them!"

"Bad times for everybody," Petrilli stated. "Many families are beginning to go hungry, *compare*, even those from our own hometown, mind you . . ."

"Yes," Jacques said, having calmed down. "In the park, just a ways up from here, the other day they said that we're in the middle of a deep crisis. But after the election, they also said, jobs will pick up again like before."

"And when will these elections take place?" Annibalini asked, anxious.

"Well, I have to go to work now," the *compare* said, picking up his keys and gathering his woolen cap from a nail on the wall. As he walked out, he motioned good-bye with a half-hearted gesture of his hand.

"Will they take place soon, Jacques?"

"In a couple of months, that's what they said over at the park."

3

Ten months had gone by since Onofrio Annibalini had arrived. And ten months had passed without the prospect of a job in sight for him.

Jacques had managed to find a job with a cleaning service organization that paid a dollar an hour. As for Onofrio, nobody wanted him. He was an older man, even paying him eighty cents an hour was a losing proposition when there were plenty of young men who were eager to work for less than that.

The harsh winter was over: the harsh Canadian winter that buries streets, houses and hope alike under ice had come and gone but work was still nowhere to be found. The prospects that were talked about at friends' houses, while sitting around the card table trying to kill time and thoughts, vanished just as dreams do at dawn.

"As soon as it thaws, as soon as the snow melts," old timers would say over and over again, "there will be work for everyone."

It had thawed quite some time ago. The snow had melted and cleared and it was the beginning of summer, but the prophecy had not yet come true. Wherever you knocked, the door remained shut.

One day Onofrio Annibalini stopped to look at a sign in a construction site. Since he didn't know how to read, another Italian job-hunter told him that it said: *Qui non c'è lavoro* (There is no work here). It was written in large and clear bold letters, and in Italian.

On the other side of the fence hundreds of men, like ants, were building a skyscraper. Chests bared and tanned all over, these ants were earning their bread for the winter that would soon be there again. Another winter with lots of snow and ice and the inevitable unemployment. Unemployment, no bread, no money, and at home the long faces of *compare* Petrilli, the *comare* and their sons who were already making it clear that they minded having him around, although at the end of each week they faithfully wrote down, in a little black book, fifteen dollars for his room and board.

Fifteen dollars a week for the last ten months. It meant that he owed them five or six hundred dollars, in addition to the cost of the work contract and of the steamship ticket. Meanwhile at construction sites all over town the signs kept on reading: *Qui non c'è lavoro* (There is no work here). In large and bold letters. And in clear Italian.

"There is no work here," Onofrio kept on thinking, imagining his *compare* sitting at the table and him listening. "And in this house, dear *compare*, there is no place for you any more. It's not my fault, you see, that you cannot find a job anywhere. And you will understand it's not my fault either if I am forced to ask you to look elsewhere for shelter. I have a family to feed, and I have my own troubles. Given that there is the *sangiovanni* between us and we are *compari*, for you I have already done enough and what you owe me is now way too much."

And he would be on his way from door to door, day after day, looking for shelter under a stairway or God only knows where.

"*Qui non c'è lavoro*" – Place Ville Marie.

"There is no work here" – rue Sainte Catherine.

"There is no work here" – Boulevard Saint Laurent.

"There is no work here" – rue Saint Dominique.

"There is no work here" – Boulevard Saint Joseph.

Onofrio Annibalini began to have dreams. A parcel of land in his hometown. A parcel of land that even in time of drought, when you spend nights dreaming of drowning in a sea of clear purifying water, can grow a stalk of hemlock for you to chew. And it tastes good, that stalk of hemlock. It tastes good because it is yours. And because it is yours it tastes better than the bowl of soup offered by the *compare* that you accept for convenience sake, that you eat for convenience sake, but which from your bowels comes back to your mouth like scalding bile every time you think about it. In that bile an invisible live toad makes you shudder in bed at night, and in the daytime, when you are out in the streets dragging your blistered stinking feet, beats you like a hammer in the head.

A live toad, yes. And it hops and it hops.

He had also knocked on the doors of sacristies. Inevitably a slick and suspicious sacristan would open up, take a good look at him then say: "The Reverend Father is out!"

He would stand there open-mouthed, each and every time. They all spoke before he had a chance to say anything. Only afterwards, when again in the streets, he would become aware of the fact that he had wanted to say this and that, perhaps even threaten in the name of the God that they were supposed to serve. But he was already alone, as always.

One day Onofrio was sitting on a bench in the Saint Zotique Park. Disheartened, eyes gazing into nothingness, he had taken off his shoes and the thick socks made of coarse wool by the old women of his hometown to massage his tired and blistered feet. As he was lacing up his shoes again, he felt the overwhelming desire to let out shrill screams full of rage that had stored up within and needed an urgent outlet. This, he thought, might help free him of those demons that kept him angry and awake at night, and made him sweat like a mare under the heat of the summer sun, carrying a load of freshly thrashed wheat from the hut in the field to the town and flicking her tail on her sweat-drenched body swimming with thousands of horseflies.

Thrashing time! A sacred annual rite that perpetuates and immortalizes the sacrifice of poor old farmers. A rite of poverty for sure, but it never failed to unfold in an atmosphere of perfect peace, joy and contentment. Piles and piles of golden wheat arranged in circles on a piece of level ground fifteen feet square; a crazy horse that turns round and round a thousand times a day, dragging a massive thrashing stone; the farmer that removes and renews his golden lode; his woman, kerchief tied around her head, sorting out the wheat; and further out, where the breeze is stronger, the children, sieve in hand, patiently separating the chaff from the wheat. And songs, songs everywhere in the valleys and in the hills, centuries old songs that were harbingers of everlasting joy.

"And you, Onofrio Annibalini, you left all that?" Annibalini reproached himself as he finished lacing up his shoes.

"Yes, yes, I did, and it's true. But I had to do it. I had to get away from Carmela," Annibalini answered to himself.

"A woman becomes public property when she starts sleeping around. You should have split her head open with an axe when she wouldn't sleep with you."

"Yes, I know. I should have," Annibalini answered to Annibalini again. "But I didn't do it."

"Why didn't you? Wouldn't jail have been better than living, as you do, in this country that's not yours?"

He had barely finished hearing his own reproaching voice when he was startled by the intrusion of someone else's voice.

"Hello, my friend," the voice said. "How did you manage to reduce yourself to such condition?"

The voice that was addressing him belonged to a man in his thirties, in shirt-sleeves but refined in manner.

"No job!" Onofrio answered brusquely, turning to stare at the church steps across to avert a second eye contact with the stranger.

"Have you been looking?" the stranger asked.

"Nooo, never! I have just been sitting on this here bench all my life," Onofrio answered bitterly.

He shifted his gaze from the stranger to one corner of the square. There was a bank, there: the beginning and the end of his dreams.

The stranger pulled out a pack of cigarettes, lit one up with an elegant lighter that went *click* when he opened it and *clack* when he closed it. He inhaled the smoke, let some out from the corners of his mouth and then some from the center puckering his lips funnel-like, as if to emphasize the great pleasure he was taking in smoking.

Onofrio Annibalini looked at the little clouds of smoke as they came out of the stranger's mouth, saw them expand in front of him and remembered the great smell of tobacco. He would have liked to stretch out a hand to grab the clouds of smoke and stop them, just as a moment earlier he had wanted to stop a thought, a dream. But then he pondered and said to himself, only the crazy can be eager to grab what's not a substance, and only dreamers live with the illusion of being able to stop a dream, a thought.

"Fact is," the stranger said, "no one cares about us Italians. How long have you been here?"

"Ten months!"

"And you never worked?"

"Never worked!"

"I can consider myself lucky," the stranger asserted. "Four months after landing, I found a good job."

"Ah!" Onofrio nodded.

The stranger was silent for a moment, while stealthily studying Onofrio's reaction to what he had said.

"And that's not all," he went on. "At the same time I came to own a piece of this blessed land, and I didn't have a red cent."

"And how did you do it?" Onofrio asked, by now, curious.

"How did I do it?" the stranger replied, still smiling. "There are kind souls here too, you know, not only in the Vatican."

"I don't believe in kind souls any more," Onofrio Annibalini said, once again looking at the church steps across the park.

"And yet, as sure as Jesus died to save mankind, I tell you that goodness still exists."

"Would you know where it might be housed?"

"You make me laugh, *paisà*," the stranger remarked, while pulling out again his pack of cigarettes and offering him one. "Here, have a smoke."

Onofrio hadn't tasted a cigarette in months. He took it and started packing it down, as he used to do with cigarettes made with tobacco trimmings he smoked in Italy. He hesitated before putting it to his lips, then heard the *click*. He felt he heat of the flame under his nose and, while inhaling the first drag, he heard the elegant *clack*.

"Thanks," he muttered.

"What for?" the young man answered. Then, after a brief pause, he added: "I don't even know you, *paisà*, but after what you just told me I feel that I have to do something to help you out."

"Talk is cheap," Onofrio sighed. "What could you possibly do for someone like me?"

"I could take you to the house of goodness. Come along," the stranger said, as he stood up. "I am taking you to see the man who got me my first job three years ago. Maybe he can do something for you too."

Onofrio hesitated. He didn't believe in miracles and was so tired that his bottom felt stuck fast to the bench. Yet he did get up. He got up and followed the stranger, as dejected and downhearted as a convalescent.

"It isn't far, just a little ways from here. But we'll take my car," the man said.

"You have a car?" Onofrio asked, as if to pay him a compliment.

"After three years, you see, it's only natural. I work, I have always worked since I met this engineer I am going to introduce you to, and I am not married. What about you, are you married?" the stranger asked, as they were approaching his big car.

"In a small town like mine, for us peasants, a wife is half the bread we will ever have. So yes," Annibalini answered, "I am married."

"Hell, half the bread!" the young man said, as he opened the car door for him. "Perhaps where you come from, my friend. But in the city, here and in Italy, doesn't matter where, a wife is a burden. And a debt."

"And yet if she works," Onofrio answered, as he sank in the comfort of the car seat, "if a woman works here, she can be the only bread you will ever have."

"That is true. It's easier for a woman to find a job. They aren't paid much, maybe sixty cents an hour. But they can find a job."

"And yet, you see, I have tried to find a job for sixty cents an hour. But no one is willing to give it to me."

The young man laughed, and started the car. They soon arrived at their destination and Onofrio was introduced into a messy old office, where he could smell the odor of money and deals.

They were cordially received by a man in his forties, who invited them to sit down and offered them both a cigarette.

"So what's new with you, Perussi?" he asked, in a tight Northern Italian accent.

"With me, nothing," Perussi answered, while looking at Onofrio.

"Are you still working where I sent you?"

"You bet I am. And last month they gave me a raise, fifteen cents an hour."

"You are doing well then."

"You bet I am, *ingegné*. I will always be grateful for everything you have done for me and my thanks come from the heart. You are a good man."

"Come on, now. Let's leave compliments out of this," the engineer said, abruptly.

While smoking the cigarette he had been offered, Onofrio listened and looked at the two men. Maybe it was true, after all! Maybe charitable souls did exist. Maybe the nicest of them all was right there, within those four walls and embodied in that man, a gentle man with such a noble way about him, a man with a wholesome smile who seemed to exude goodness from his very eyes.

"This is a friend of mine," Perussi said. "He has been here for ten months, but no work. He is my *paesano*, I ran into him a little while ago as he was despairing because no one is willing to give him a job."

"He is rather old for this young country," the engineer said, "and probably without skills. I can see why no one wants to give him a job."

"That's the way I see it," Onofrio said, apologetically. "Who would want to give this old man a job?"

"And yet, *ingegné*," Perussi retorted, trying to be convincing, "you could do something for him, if you wanted."

"It's not a question of me wanting or not wanting, Perussi," the engineer answered, resting his elbows on the desk. "Of course I want to be of help to your friend. But do you know how many unemployed people there are so far this year?"

"I heard three or four hundred thousand in Quebec."

"And eight or nine hundred thousand in all of Canada," the engineer remarked, interrupting him.

"This notwithstanding, *ingegné*," Perussi repeated, with a confident smile, "I know that you will do something for my *paesano*. He has a wife and children in Italy who have been waiting ten months for the first dollar to arrive!"

"I see. Well, I'll think of something."

When Onofrio heard these words, he felt relieved. "He will think of something," he thought. "It means that tonight I can eat in peace. And that in a little while I may even be able to tell the *compare* that I'll start to pay rent and pay off my debt."

"But now," the good engineer continued, "in the spur of the moment, I cannot promise anything. I will speak with the head of the development company to see what can be done."

"I'll kiss your feet, *ingegné*," said Onofrio, filled with emotion, a rush of joy going through his heart. "I'll be grateful to you for the rest of my life."

"Don't mention it, my good man. We are all Italians after all. Leave your phone number with me, I'll call you this evening to let you know something."

Onofrio pulled a piece of paper out of his pocket with the Petrilli's address and phone number. He handed it over to the engineer who took note of it on his pad, then gave it back to him.

4

When Onofrio got back home that afternoon, the *comare*
Michelina was intent at preparing dinner. None of the
men were back yet.

In spite of her age, the *comare* was still in good wom-
anly shape. A plump and saucy behind, a full pair of tits
that dangled like those of the black women he had known
during his months in the African campaign, and which
were not supported by a bra, from which they would
have burst out in any case. And her thighs! On more than
one occasion Onofrio had eyed out those thighs while she
was bent over looking in the refrigerator, and had re-
awakened in him the forgotten fire of lust.

On those occasions he would have liked to ask her
not to move from the open refrigerator, or to lean onto a
chair as if to look at a nail that was sticking out of it.

He knew that his feelings sprang in part from the
desire of revenge, because his *compare*'s family had done
nothing to help him find a job. But he also knew that the
comare reminded him of his wife. Not physically, though,
but rather because she too had slept around after the
compare had first left for Canada. Women do that, and the
comare was just another woman.

Onofrio rid his mind of these thoughts, suddenly
considering them unworthy of him. He told the *comare*
that he was waiting for a call, perhaps the good one, and
went into the living room where the phone was. He sat
down, nervous and brooding, while in the other room the
comare continued to do her chores without making too
much noise. Only now and then could he hear a cabinet

door slam and once a metal object fell to the floor and made him jump.

Then the phone rang. Onofrio had his hand on it and picked it up in a flash. It was Jacques. He was calling to say that he would be working the night shift as well and would not be coming home at all. The *compare* Petrilli and his other son, Domenico, came home soon after that and they ate in silence, as they usually did lately.

Onofrio was hesitant, he couldn't decide whether or not to talk openly about the slim hope he had been given. In the end he decided to say nothing; the *comare* knew and it was enough. For all he knew, the whole thing could have ended up in smoke, just like other times. So he said nothing, just sat there musing while his food and his thoughts were blended into a poisonous mixture.

That evening the phone didn't ring again. It rang the following morning around ten, while Onofrio was on the front porch watching some kids at play in the alley and trying to keep ugly thoughts out of his mind. But it was as if all the thoughts that were driving him crazy were nailed fast in the lining of his head, like flies sucking blood and pus from a wound.

"I have spoken to the boss at the construction company," the engineer said, when he later received Onofrio in his office. "He told me that they could hire another worker at the site of the new construction downtown."

"Thank you, *ingegné.* You really are a good man."

"He could hire you," the engineer interrupted, "but there is of course one condition."

"*Ingegné,* if there is something to pay, anything at all, I'll pay. I'll borrow the money and pay. A debt more, a debt less, it makes no difference now. If I work I can pay off my debts, but if I don't, I'll just make others that I won't be able to ever repay."

"That's how things are," the engineer said, with a sigh. "Alas, that's indeed how things are even though it hurts to have to admit it."

For a moment they both stood silent, looking each other in the eyes. Onofrio didn't know what to say. He just waited in the knowledge that his fate was in the hands of the engineer. He felt lost, subconsciously knowing that he would do everything, anything the man would ask him to do.

"Well then," the engineer concluded. "This is the deal. The development company is not asking for money to give you a job. It is a serious and important company. But since they have land to sell in order to develop an area in the outskirts of town, they would like you to buy a lot valued at eight hundred dollars. Then they will hire you in one of their construction jobs."

"Eight hundred dollars!" Onofrio sighed.

"Eight hundred dollars," the engineer confirmed. "However, you have to keep in mind that in a year or so the area will be thoroughly developed and your lot will be worth double that or triple, quadruple. God only knows how much more it will be worth."

"But if . . ." Onofrio tried to say.

"There are no buts and no ifs," he was brusquely cut off. "You do not understand. The interest of the company is simply this: there are no homes in that area and only a few lots have been sold so far. If they can show that a good number of lots have been sold, they can hike the price and make much more money on the property that is left. Now they practically give the lots away for eight hundred dollars, one to you, one to me, one to someone else. But in due time they will get eight thousand dollars for just one of the remaining lots and they will make hundreds of thousands of dollars. Do you understand now?"

"Oh!" Onofrio smiled, naively. "Pretty shrewd, aren't they? Now I see where the trick is!"

"Great. I am happy that you understand," the engineer said, winking in agreement.

"You have to have one hell of a brain to be in business. Who could have ever imagined?"

"Very clever, aren't they?" the engineer agreed, indulging him.

"Very clever indeed, *ingegné*. When you are born a *cafone*, you die a *cafone*."

"So what do you want me to tell them?"

"*Ingegné*, I have to find the money. Will they give me the time it takes to borrow it?"

"Well, all I have to do is pass on the message. But the deal, do you like the deal?"

"Of course I do. I like it. I just hope I can find the money."

"Do you think you can?"

"I think so. There are so many people from back home, here," Onofrio said. "If I borrow a few dollars from each one of them, I should be able to get to eight hundred dollars in just a few days."

"Add about eighty more for the lawyer, because the lawyer is paid by the buyer. But you knew that, didn't you?"

"Of course. But I hadn't thought of that."

The begging for the loan was long and painful. For country people like Onofrio Annibalini, the greatest pains to bear are not the physical ones but the moral ones.

"I must be humble, ever so humble," Onofrio kept on repeating to himself, over and over again during those days, as he went from door to door asking the more fortunate of his hometown friends for a loan, no matter how small. "It is the price one must pay, here, to get blessed satisfaction later. One has to suffer and suffer, bear burdens beyond endurance. But it will be all the more beautiful when you can enjoy life and walk head high. What a suffering this is! Will I ever be able to see the end of the tunnel?"

He had managed to gather four hundred dollars from people from his hometown, who lent him the money on his word at fifteen percent interest. He needed five hundred more.

When the *compare* Petrilli found out from others what was going on, he made Onofrio Annibalini a business proposition: he would lend him the five hundred dollars he needed, provided that for these and for the rest of the money he owed him, he would agree to mortgage the undivided estate of his deceased father as collateral, with a yearly interest add-on of fifteen percent.

Onofrio accepted the *compare*'s offer. There was nothing else he could do, and he knew it. He got someone to help him draft a letter to Michele Scardocchia, his proxy, to inform him of the move he was about to make, and to ask him to send the required papers.

5

When the mortgage papers were all drawn up and sent to Italy to be recorded, Onofrio Annibalini thought that his troubles had come to an end.

It didn't turn out to be that way.

It didn't, because his brother Pasquale sued him, in Italy, requesting that the estate be subdivided between them. He contended that he could not, in his own heart, continue to be the co-owner of a property that had been mortgaged for nearly two million *lire*, as this soiled the memory of their deceased father. The relevant papers were submitted by the Court of Larino and served to "Michele Scardocchia, as Proxy for Onofrio Annibalini."

It was the end of October. Michele Scardocchia was harvesting olives when the Server from Casacalenda, delegated by the Court of Larino, arrived at his farm.

"Are you Michele Scardocchia?" the man asked, with a thick Neapolitan accent.

"Yes, I am," Scardocchia answered, while coming down the ladder that was leaning against an olive tree.

"And you, Mister Scardocchia, you are the Proxy for Mister Onofrio Annibalini?"

"At your service, *signore*."

"A summons is being served by the Court of Larino," the Court officer blurted out. Then, without giving him a chance to ask for details, he added: "Here is a faithful copy of the original. I shall mark it as personally delivered to Michele Scardocchia, Proxy for Onofrio Annibalini, on October 24, 1959. Good day, sir."

As soon as he finished jotting down the annotation, the officer handed him the summons and went away.

Michele Scardocchia was dumbstruck and just stood there, staring at the papers and turning them around in his hands. He didn't even have the time to say good-bye to the man.

He went to the hut, put his glasses on and started reading the papers. Only then did he realize what the whole thing was all about.

That very evening, back in town, he went to Pasquale Annibalini's house to find out if they could come to some sort of reasonable agreement. Pasquale was having dinner. He welcomed Scardocchia kindly and offered him a glass of wine. However, when he realized why Scardocchia had come to his house, his face darkened.

"I don't talk about these things with friends," he said sternly. "That's why I have put everything in the hands of a lawyer. I pay him to serve me, and he will do whatever is necessary to protect my interests. If you want to talk about these things, you should go see him. You are now a guest in my house, I offer you a glass of wine because we are old friends, but we cannot talk about these things."

Once he had spoken his piece, Pasquale Annibalini locked himself in an absolute silence and resumed eating without raising his head. He spoke again only to answer Scardocchia who, having finished his glass of wine, said good-bye and left, tail tucked between his legs.

Fully aware of the responsibility he had assumed when Onofrio Annibalini named him his proxy, Michele Scardocchia decided to go personally to the Court in Larino and take stock of the situation before incurring the expense to engage a lawyer.

The following morning he got up very early. He had to walk all the way to Signalman's House Number 50, where certain local trains stopped to pick up passengers from Provvidenti. As usual, he calmly made the necessary preparations for the long walk and for making himself presentable in Court.

It wasn't the first time he went to Larino, he knew the town well. As soon as he got there, his briefcase firmly tucked under arm, he went downtown and stopped for a coffee at the Court House. He stopped a moment at the foot of the long stairway that led to the upper floors of the Court House, then began his climb at a slow, dignified pace, head high in admiration.

Portly, elegantly dressed in his blue suit, starched white shirt and multicolored bow-tie, newly polished shoes, his elegant leather briefcase tightly held under his arm, with a gentle bow he greeted everyone he met up the stairway and along the hallways and everyone greeted him back respectfully.

He walked up to the usher and stopped.

"Good morning," he said. "Anyone in yet?"

"Of course everyone is in," the usher replied, without lifting his eyes from the pages of *Il Mondo Giudiziario*. Then, without stopping his reading, he asked: "May I help you?"

"My name is Michele Scardocchia. I am the pro . . ."

"Oh, sorry, sir," the usher apologized, interrupting him. He got up at once and, hastily folding his newspaper, explained: "We were not expecting you today, sir. But please make yourself at home. I'll call the Court Clerk immediately. This way, please."

He escorted Michele Scardocchia to an office marked *Prosecutor's Office*, while bowing repeatedly on the way. He opened the door, insisted that Michele Scardocchia enter first, then withdrew in great haste but not before he had repeated, once more: "With apologies, sir. I shall call the Court Clerk now."

Michele Scardocchia had not expected to be looked after with such care, nor did he expect so many obsequious bows of respect. Indeed, he did not even expect to be escorted into such an elegant office.

The massive walnut desk, the grand carved shelving stacked with the dusty books that held the secrets of law and order, the stuffed chairs symmetrically arranged around the desk: these were things he had only dreamed about.

None of this had he expected. It was all a dream. And as if to give his dream substance, transfixed, he walked around the desk and sat down. He sank into the soft leather chair, leaned against its back rest and closed his eyes. In his heart he gave a million thanks to Onofrio Annibalini for having given him the opportunity to be treated like a gentleman by these fine people at the Court of Larino.

He heard a knock at the door – he wasn't expecting the Court Clerk to knock before entering – and was surprised by the warm, mellow tone his voice took on, a voice that didn't sound like his at all, when he answered: "Please, come in!"

The door opened and a short fat man, glasses low on the bridge of his nose, round head crowned by grey hair like an old monk waddled forward.

"Good morning, Mr. Prosecutor," he said.

Michele Scardocchia sunk deep into his extraordinary dream. The little man came forward, extending his pudgy soft hand across the desk.

"Good morning, Mr. Prosecutor," the short fat man repeated, with humility and solicitude. Then, halfway smiling, he added: "I am the Court Clerk and I have been here for fifteen years. You know, I am now a bit like a father to our young Recorders and Investigators who come and go restlessly, always complaining that they don't like it here in Larino. But what can we expect, they're all so very young. They'll be coming in shortly to meet you, sir. And I hope that you will enjoy the refreshments that we and the people in Magistrate Court have arranged to welcome you in our Halls of Justice."

"Gladly," Michele Scardocchia surprised himself once more with the subdued tone of his voice. "I must say you are all truly kind here."

"Modestly, sir. With your permission," the Clerk said, bowing and making his way towards the door which he opened while cautiously looking out.

There was an unusual excitement just outside the door. Michele Scardocchia could hear hurried steps and the muffled voice of people coming and going. The Clerk made a gesture with his head and one by one a dozen or so employees filtered in and shook hands with Scardocchia, as he remained seated at the desk like a king.

"D'Addario, Head Court Recorder."

"Ragazzini, Process Server."

"D'Amico, Court Recorder."

"Signorini, Magistrate Court."

And so on and so on. Michele Scardocchia had a kind, reassuring smile for each one of them, all the while feeling himself lost and small but also infinitely happy in that unreal world that engulfed him like a jewel in a velvet-lined box.

Soon after, two waiters came in. Scardocchia recognized one of them as the waiter who earlier had served him coffee at the Bar downstairs. He had been rather discourteous, if truth be known. Now he eyed him out of the corner of his eye, a bit ashamed, his silence seeming to speak out an apology, "I'm sorry, sir. I really didn't know!"

When it was all over, after the toasts were made and everyone had offered their good wishes, wishes that

Michele Scardocchia didn't understand or even hear, he found himself alone once again with the Court Clerk. The little man with the monk-like round head started talking about legal matters, the laws, articles of the Civil and Criminal Codes, Civil and Criminal procedures, but never once did he make reference to the Annibalini estate. It was at this point that a suspicion began to take root in his mind.

While the Clerk kept on talking, Michele Scardocchia was already trying to think of a way to get out of the situation before digging himself in any deeper.

He considered being honest and saying that he was merely the proxy of a friend who had emigrated to Canada, and that they certainly had mistaken him for someone else. But at the mere thought of doing that he saw himself being beaten and hand-cuffed like a common criminal by the same kind people who had treated him like a king just a while before.

While considering the situation, he felt hot flashes on his face. He began sweating and fidgeting nervously. The chair, comfortable and reassuring a moment ago, now felt hot enough to burn his bottom.

As the Court Clerk went on and on about articles of the Codes and procedures, Michele Scardocchia could only nod yes and no but always in absolute panic. In the end the Court Clerk got tired, stopped yapping, said good-bye and left.

Finally alone but nailed to the leather chair, Michele Scardocchia didn't know what to do. Then suddenly in panic he stood up, took his briefcase and walked out, silently closing the door behind him. In the hallways there were only a few country folks sitting on the wooden benches and talking, their lunch wrapped up in checkered napkins and held under arm.

He managed to flee, unnoticed, down the stairs and out of the building.

He didn't wait for the bus to take him to the railroad station, nor did he wait for the train. He headed straight for the State Road in the opposite direction, having decided to walk all the way back home as a penance, or perhaps in order to have the time to better think how he might explain to all concerned what had happened. Or maybe he just knew that he had to leave town as soon as possible.

He arrived in Casacalenda in good time, already knowing what he had to do next. He would go to the Notary's office and formally renounce his power of attorney.

That's exactly what he did before going back to Providenti where, comfortably seated at the kitchen table, he drafted two letters: one to Onofrio, one to the Court Clerk of Larino.

To his friend, he explained the situation as best as he could. In closing, he told him that his state of mind was such that he lacked the clear judgment necessary to continue being his proxy. He asked him to understand, if he altogether could, and to forgive him.

To the Court Clerk, he wrote an anonymous letter in which he explained that the Prosecutor they had so warmly welcomed and whose arrival they had so elegantly celebrated in the great Halls of Justice was merely the poor and unsuspecting proxy of a farmer who had emigrated to Canada and knew nothing about Civil and Criminal Codes and procedures. The whole affair, he concluded, must have been a case of mistaken identity. If so, he hoped that they would find their own way to justify his actions as well as theirs.

6

When Onofrio Annibalini finished listening to the reading of his friend's letter, he couldn't even get upset. He was perfectly in peace with himself, now that he had started working. He was earning sixty to seventy dollars a week, depending on the hours he put in; and he was determined to allow nothing to interfere with the rest of his happy life. As far as he was concerned, the matter could end up however God and man's justice willed.

He had started paying off his debts a little at a time, and had even sent some money home to his wife. He figured that if he kept up sending around thirty dollars a month back home, his wife would be happy, he would be free of worries while paying off his debts, and he would even be able to put a few dollars in the bank.

Four months had passed since he had started working. *Compare* Petrilli and his family were now treating him better. They even greeted him with a nice smile when he came back home from work in the evening. He was paying them fifteen dollars a week for room and board, and twenty five dollars, some times even more, towards his loan.

His job was quite easy, not at all dangerous like that of many of his companions who worked perched up high on the walls of the skyscraper under construction. From the ground up, his co-workers looked small like squirrels, and like squirrels they moved on walls and girders.

He had struck a nice friendship with one of these workers, whose name was Peppe. Like him, Peppe was from a small southern town in Italy and they learned to love and respect each other as if they were old friends, indeed as if they were childhood friends.

Onofrio had been working at the construction job about four months, and he had been a friend of Peppe's for an equal amount of time when his friend became the victim of a terrible accident.

Sirens from ambulances could suddenly be heard from every direction. Like always, they made his blood curdle. Every time sirens went off in the city, they made his blood curdle just like the first time he heard them, the time of the Saint Jerome affair.

The Saint Jerome tragedy must have had its roots in unemployment. That's what everyone said at the time, and it was probably true.

"Why in the hell does trouble always find only us Italians?" Onofrio asked himself.

Maybe Bob Perussi had been right when, some time back, he had told him that no one cares about Italians, no one gives them a helping hand. The biggest disappointments didn't come from foreigners who, although not inclined to help, weren't likely to hurt you either, but from Italians themselves. Bob wasn't the only one who had told him this. "Because of the all-mighty dollar, even brothers and sisters have lost love and respect for one another," the *comare* Michelina had told him one day. "Just think, last year when her sister arrived from Italy, my friend Eva took a day off from work to help her find a job. They found one soon enough, but since the pay was better than where she worked, Eva told her sister that they were looking for someone who knew how to speak a bit of English. So she quit her old job and, though she speaks no English at all, she took the new while her sister ended up jobless for over two months."

Jacques chimed in: "Don't even think about going to the Casa d'Italia for help. You'll find a sour old spinster who snarls at you, and if you don't keep your fists tightly clenched in your pockets, you'll end up choking the old broad. It has happened to me, honest to God. Assistance, assistance, they say. Assistance, my foot! Only God could be of assistance, and even then."

"Leave God out of this, my son," his father interrupted him. "He has already done His job once and, as the old saying goes, God only helps those who help themselves. So keep on going and sweating, *così è la vita*." Yes. They were probably right, all of them. Otherwise God, if He still accounted for anything at all in this world, would have arranged things differently in Saint Jerome.

He wouldn't have put two unemployed men under the same roof, two strangers who only had two things in common: the younger was engaged to the daughter of the older one, and both were unemployed that winter.

The younger man, Mike, having nothing else to do was always at the girl's house. He was a grabby sort and kept on touching the girl right in front of mother and father with the excuse that he was a modern man, *all'americana,*as he boasted.

"Listen, young man," his future father-in-law told him one day. "You can touch my daughter as much as you want when you marry her, but not now. You spend the whole damn day in my house with your hands all over her. Good thing that I am not working and can keep an eye on you, otherwise by now Rosanna would be walking around with a shameful belly. When you are in my house, and this is my house, young man, remember, you keep your hands to yourself. If you cannot, that's the door over there."

Mike chose to play at being offended. For two weeks he stayed away, and when the girl called him, he had others tell her that he wasn't home. One day however, after mass, he ran into mother and daughter across the Church Madonna della Difesa on Dante Street. The mother convinced him to let bygones be bygones.

"You shouldn't take offense," she told him. "A father is a father, someday you'll understand. When his daughter grows up and becomes a woman, he starts thinking. Maybe he remembers how he was at her age and thinks she is the same way now. His desires, when he was young, in his mind are the daughter's desires, and he knows that it takes only a match to start up the fire."

The woman managed to convince Mike. And since he really loved Rosanna and wanted to marry her, he made peace with the family.

On that very day he went back to the house and stayed for lunch, as he had done so many other times before. As for the master of the house, he didn't seem to mind and after some time he even resumed making idle chat while remaining somewhat cold and indifferent, but watching over his women in a way that Mike had never seen before.

A few days went by. Mike was back to his grabby habits and Rosanna's father started making scenes again.

"Marry her, for Christ's sake," he yelled out one day. "Marry my daughter, don't make a whore out of her."

"But how can we?" his daughter said. "How can we marry and set up house if Mike cannot find a job?"

"What's wrong with this house?" her father replied, since his greatest concern was to see his daughter married off before she remained a spinster or turned up pregnant. "You are my only daughter, and as there is food for three, there can be food for four while it lasts."

That was all Mike wanted to hear. He rushed fast after that and even had the wedding date set in a hurry. The thought of the upcoming wedding, however, must have gone to his head because he began to behave as if he were the master of something or other and became more amorous and more blatant in his advances toward Rosanna.

One day, the father-in-law-to-be surprised Mike as he kissed the daughter first and then the mother. He lost his head and a kitchen knife took the life of all three. A match set the house ablaze, dead bodies and all.

He went to the police station to give himself up and simply said: "I had to do it to save my honor."

Everyone knew that unemployment had been the real cause of the tragedy. When people are idle, they acquire bad habits and, through the acquired bad habits, they seek to forget their boredom.

This happened soon after Onofrio had arrived in Canada and the sirens went crazy: those of the ambulances, those of the police cars, and those of the fire engines.

This time, the sirens had gone off for his friend Peppe, even though there was no way that Onofrio could have known it yet. They stopped their whining on the opposite side of the construction site and Onofrio ran up with other workers. He was told that his friend Peppe had been burned to death way up there. He had been working on a metal scaffolding when this came in contact with a high tension wire. Peppe and an Irish man died instantly while two others, a French-Canadian and a Sicilian, had the presence of mind to jump onto a lower scaffolding, thus saving their lives.

After the accident, the Sicilian who had been able to save himself said to Onofrio: "I suddenly saw a flash above me, and Peppe's face became white. I saw flames coming out of his chest. Yes, out of his very chest, flames. And Peppe, poor soul, he just had the time to scream. He screamed and fell, from the scaffolding to the ground."

"My God. Oh my God," Onofrio said. "What am I going to do? How am I going to tell his wife?"

"Where is she?" the Sicilian asked, still overcome by fear as he lay on the stretcher awaiting to be taken away.

"She was supposed to come out of the hospital today. Peppe was supposed to have picked her up in the afternoon."

"If only he had gone! Listen, I am not going to work here anymore. I am going to stop working in construction and go back to tailoring. I'll earn less, but I won't be endangering my life."

After the initial questioning, they took him away together with the bodies of the unfortunate workers. Then the foreman was questioned by the police.

"The men had received specific instructions," the foreman said. "They were not to touch any metal object over there."

"That isn't true!" one of the workers yelled out. It was the man who had been working on the scaffolding with the Sicilian and who had saved himself by jumping down. "It isn't at all true. Let me tell you, there are killings and killings, but one of the worst forms of murder is to allow us workers to be exposed to this kind of danger."

"Okay, okay. Say what you wish but don't make accusations," the foreman said defensively. "There will be an official investigation, isn't that so?" he then asked the Police Inspector. "Isn't it true that there will be an official investigation to determine who is responsible for this?"

The Police Inspector acknowledged his agreement with a nod of the head, then instructed his men to maintain order and to drive off the workers and the onlookers.

"If you are undertaking a serious investigation," another one of the workers said while a policeman was trying to push him away, "remember that there have been three other fatalities on this job. And don't forget the man who fell from the fourteenth floor last March, due to inadequate protection."

The truth of the matter is that in that and similar other construction projects, budgeted at a cost of millions of dollars, even the most basic safety devices would have been sufficient to prevent accidents. A properly insulated wire doesn't cost much more than one that isn't, with the difference that a cheap wire is a real hazard for those who work near it on a scaffolding.

There was no excuse, there couldn't be any: it was blatant negligence, sheer ambition to quickly complete one project in order to be able to move on to another. It was neglect that caused disasters that were avoidable and not at all necessary for the successful completion of a work of art such as the skyscraper.

No. It was not a simple accident. It was a disaster caused by neglect and carelessness and the Italians, who always accepted the most dangerous jobs either to make more money or simply because they were the only jobs offered to them, who very often were the victims.

When Onofrio arrived at Peppe's house, his wife was not there. She had been informed of the accident by the police and, weak as she was, she fainted and had to be taken back to the hospital. Onofrio went there right away, to be of comfort to his friend's wife.

As soon as the woman saw him, she hugged him, leaned her head on his shoulder and began to cry like a woman possessed. Onofrio didn't know what to say to calm her down. He held her tight against his chest with one hand, and with the other he stroked her head as if he wanted, with that gesture, to promise a replacement for the protection she had just lost: a protection that neither he, nor the few meager dollars of the insurance company could possibly ever give her.

7

After Peppe's accident, Onofrio Annibalini worked on that same construction job for another two weeks. Then snow fell, everything froze again and hundreds of workers were laid off. The hardest hit were those who worked outside, who resumed their "Stations of the Cross" hunting down jobs.

When not out job hunting, this miserable lot of human wrecks stood in line at the door of the Unemployment Office to collect their pittance. Onofrio had the surprise of his life when he found out that he couldn't even avail himself of this meager unemployment benefit, because he had not worked long enough to qualify.

"Why don't you join the *furnaciare* and go shovel snow?" *compare* Petrilli told him one day. "You're bound to make some little money. They pay as much as a dollar an hour, and if you work ten hours a day, that's ten dollars, and you have enough to eat for a week."

"I'll go. Of course I'll go, *compare*. But where do I find these *furnaciare*?"

"You'll have to stand on street corners," Dominique said. "They drive by with the snow-trucks, they pick you up and take you God knows where, on the highways or along the railroads tracks, or through city streets. It doesn't matter, that's what they do, year after year."

On the following morning, Onofrio Annibalini got up at five full of hope. He put on heavy and warm clothing and went to stand on the main street corner.

There were no cars in sight at that early hour of the morning, but he stood motionless under a doorway as if he were glued there. After a little while he could hardly move, stiff as a board from the chill. He was shivering, his eyes tearing from the cold. As the tears formed, they froze right under his eyelids and down his face. His nose started running but he didn't dare take his frozen hands out of the pockets to wipe the droplets off. Only now and then he would stick his tongue out to lick the drops off.

It wasn't even snowing any more. For the first time since he had set foot in Canada, Onofrio found himself complaining to the heavens that it wasn't snowing. A strong, cold wind froze the air in his lungs and made it impossible for him to breathe. He decided that he should move. Slowly at first, as if afraid that fast motion might break his joints, he started to walk: fast and then faster, in the vain hope of warming up his limbs which he could no longer feel below the knees.

"That sonofabitch had promised me work for a whole year," he thought, "and I have only worked four and a half months. Either he finds me another job, or I'll split his head open."

He went to the engineer's office and was met by an elderly lady who just stood there, looking compassionately at him. He asked to speak with the engineer but she didn't answer, only gave knowing glances at her co-workers before looking at him again.

"I am sorry," she said. "That man isn't here any more."

"Do you know where I might find him?"

"God only knows where he is. He went away a couple of months ago," she said. "He left three months of rent unpaid. Someone said he died or something, but I really don't know for sure."

"But . . ." Onofrio said, his mouth agape, speechless.

"Yes?"

Onofrio stood there paralyzed, not knowing what to do or what to say any more.

"Eight hundred dollars," he said, after a while. He started to go away, then turned around and asked: "Where is the Italian Consulate?"

"They won't be able to do anything for you at the Consulate," a blond young man with a Florentine accent said.

"How do you know?"

"You are not the first to come looking for this so-called engineer. I know what this is all about," the blond man said. "You bought a worthless plot of land after he promised you a job. Isn't that so?"

"Yes!"

"They won't be able to do anything for you at the Consulate," the young man said again with sorrow.

"Maybe so. But just the same, could you write the address on a piece of paper for me?"

"Sure," said the young man.

Onofrio took the piece of paper with the address on it, said thanks and walked out.

Out there, it was still chilling cold.

Part Two

1

It was a peaceful evening in late May, 1959. During the past few days, stories had been published in the local papers that quickly became the talk of the town. They talked about them in offices, in factories, at construction jobs and in the homes where jobless immigrants usually gathered after supper to pass the time, to wait for a favorite TV program to air, or just to wait for bed time.

Some people thought that big shake-ups were going to take place as a result of these events. Others could swear that nothing at all would happen, as usual. At the most, some no-name gangsters might be shipped out for a change of air. One way or the other, most assured, a clean sweep would be made of Cosa Nostra in Montreal: for sure, this time!

A week earlier, a time bomb had gone off on a luxury yacht that belonged to the Curtesi brothers. The yacht had been moored at a private dock in a rather unsavory and isolated marina, up north on the Saint Lawrence River, not far from the city. There weren't any victims, but the event could not be ignored. Police cars were assigned to patrol the docks and the immediate vicinity, on Sainte Catherine and on Saint Laurent streets, places where things were likely to happen in retaliation.

Precautions notwithstanding, a few days later the Copacabana Night Club was devoured by flames. On the one hand, the police were happy about the fire because they were well aware of what that place represented for the mob. On the other hand, they could not ignore the fact that the bombing of the Curtesi's yacht and the Copacabana fire were related. As a result, the Montreal mafia was left with very few choices: it could start a family war, as it had done so many other times in the past; it could dissolve altogether, at least for a while; or it could relocate. The latter was what most everyone hoped for.

It was night fall. One of the luxury houses on Côte des Neiges was slowly being swallowed by darkness. Once in a while a car would quietly roll in and park curb-side or in the front yard. Dark figures came out and approached the house. The surroundings were very quiet, or maybe only seemed to be. The usual street chatter of the late afternoon had ceased. Suburbia had just finished watering the lawns, and porch lights were being lit one by one. Soon the street lamps would be lighting up.

In the vast cellar of the mansion there was a lot of movement and confusion that night. Waiters dressed in full regalia served whiskeys and Martinis. Pipe and cigar smoke filled the room. Everyone's attention was focused on two men, both fairly short in stature but well dressed in elegant blue striped suits. They walked back and forth impatiently in the opposite direction of each other. While pacing the floor, they only raised their head to look each new arrival in the face. Their glance was sharp and piercing, like the blade of a dagger, their eyes shifty and cunning.

They were the Curtesi brothers, and they had something else in common: a certain something that was noticeable in the way they moved and held their stance; it was their powerful and arrogant personality, a trait that instilled fear and respect. It wasn't hard to envision that a rash move, even if not violent in intent, could have an effect no less drastic than a thunderbolt striking a bull.

Everyone knew the Curtesi brothers in Montreal. They were hated and feared, some people appreciated them and others despised them. But there were also many who truly loved them. The police, on the other hand, would have paid good money to get proof damaging enough to throw both of them in jail and throw the keys away. They would rid themselves of a vexing headache and at the same time they would get a taste of sweet revenge. As things stood at the moment, the police were forced to treat the Curtesis as upstanding Canadian citizens. The general public considered them rich, respected industrialists, albeit notoriously feared by those who had to deal with them.

A strange assemblage of people surrounded the Curtesi brothers in the cellar of their luxurious Côte des Neiges mansion. Many did not even know one another. Some had come from Canadian cities from coast to coast to attend that very important meeting, others from the United States. There were longshoremen and white collar workers, hoods and naive looking individuals, the week and the strong, well dressed people and shabby looking ones. Each had been hand picked by either of the Curtesi brothers for a specific job, crucial to the operation of the organization. They spoke as little as possible, but smoked and drank a lot, and when the gaze of one of the brothers fell on any of them, they stood motionless, paralyzed. They knew that the brothers could always look deep into their eyes and reach the deepest secrets of their souls.

The bell rang again, two more people were admitted into the cellar. Soon after, John and Nick Curtesi walked to a desk and stood behind it, next to each other. Everyone quieted down and put out their pipes or cigars. Everyone looked in the direction of the brothers, waiting for one of them to open the meeting. They all knew that what they had to say amounted to an order that, in critical times such as those, had to be followed to the letter, without remarks or complaints.

Finally the younger of the two brothers, Nick Curtesi, started speaking.

"Gentlemen, I suppose you all know, or suspect, why we called you here tonight." He stopped, as if he were expecting an answer from someone in the audience. As no one uttered a word, he continued: "Once again you are here to receive certain orders. This time, however, they are not orders for a specific plan or action."

After the long silence that had served as background to the Curtesi's pacing back and forth in the cellar, the guests resumed whispering. Some started relighting their pipes and cigars, some had picked up their drinks, others yet looked impatient, concerned.

"Gentlemen," Nick Curtesi continued, and the room quieted down once again. "We will be handing out some envelopes. In them you will find money, even though you shouldn't need any. You will also find a plane ticket for a specific destination and a set of instructions which you must follow to the letter. Some of you will stay where you are, others will have to get out of circulation and reach the locations indicated. As always, you can rest assured that in a few months, a year at the most, you will receive a new set of orders together with more money and another airline ticket. It will become clear to you at that time that we will see each other again, that we will work like old times once again. That's all."

"Past Muscolo," shouted out the other Curtesi, his voice loud enough to be heard above the din of the crowd at the unexpected news.

A heavy set man came forward, picked up his envelope and quickly placed it in his pocket, unopened. He bowed good-bye and went away.

"Frank Picaro."

"Ed Spada."

"Ralph Murphy."

"Mat Cocciola."

"Nick Mansano."

Daylight was beginning to shine on the elegant mansion. The cars that had been parked in the neighboring streets and on Côte des Neiges had disappeared. Down in the cellar John and Nick Curtesi, tired and sleepy, were bringing their meeting to a close. Only one man was still there, a man in his forties with reddish blond hair and blue eyes who had been, over the years, the Curtesi's must trusted lieutenant.

"Fred," Nick Curtesi said to the man. "You will stay. We are going to pass on to you a responsibility that is presently on its way to us from Italy. Here," he added, handing him a photograph.

"And who is he?" Fred asked, perplexed.

"He is the only family we have," Nick Curtesi replied. "Our only nephew. He arrives in a few days on the *Irpinia*."

"He is our sister's son, she died when he was ten," John Curtesi said. "We had put him in a boarding school in Rome but from what the Principal tells us, we have to conclude that he does not like books very much. Anyway, he is coming to stay with us."

"Unfortunately, when he gets here his uncles will not be around!" Fred concluded. Then, examining the photograph closely, he said: "Good looking young man, isn't he?"

"A good looking boy indeed," Nick Curtesi agreed.

"Damn woman!" his brother John said, worried mad. "Damn woman! Just because her husband died on her during the war, she didn't have to wrap herself up in a black dress and cry from morning till night kneeling on the cold marble floors of her church. Christ almighty, money she did not need, and she did have a son and property to take care of. She just had to go on and kill herself, a life wasted in a sea of tears. She just had to die and put us in this predicament."

John Curtesi was getting it all out. He was freeing himself of a burden he had carried inside for too long. Once he finished saying his piece, he resumed pacing back and forth in the room. During his diatribe his brother Nick and Fred just listened with infinite patience.

"Come on now," Nick said finally. "When Roberto said he wanted to come here you were very happy, you jumped up and down at the thought of having family with you. You even said that Roberto could be for us the son we never had. Isn't that so?"

"Yeah, I guess you are right. That's what I said all right. Maybe I just feel a bit edgy – who knows? – like a father waiting for the doctor to peer from behind a hospital door and say: It's a boy it's a boy!"

"So you see, Fred," Nick said. "You see what Roberto means to us. Hard to admit we have come to think of him as our son. And now that he is coming, we have to entrust him to your care because we aren't going to be here. Do you understand what that means, Fred?" he asked, as if to make sure that Fred had gotten the full sense of his words. Then he added: "You are not in need of money, nor will you ever be. You know what you can and what you cannot do here in Montreal. You are not stupid, so don't let them catch you with the hands in the till. You know we have all the trust in the world in you, we believe in you, eh?"

"This house," John Curtesi added, while Fred looked around questioningly, as if to let the brothers understand that he wanted to know if they intended to have their nephew live there, "this house will stay locked up until we figure out what to do with it, or what to do altogether. You know that it has to be that way, and why. So you have to figure out where to settle the boy. We only ask that you take good care of him, don't leave him alone, keep a watchful eye over him, don't let him get into any trouble. He is young, and young people do dumb things."

"Don't let him get too far away from you, understand?" Nick pointed out forcefully. "We want to find him here when we come back. If we decide not to come back, we want him to be with you when you come join us."

"Very well," Fred said, while getting up to shake hands with the brothers.

He took a couple of envelopes that they handed him, and smiled. The Curtesis smiled too. They got up to accompany Fred to the door, who remained all alone in the stillness of the immense villa.

2

As was always the case when a transatlantic liner was expected, the Port of Montreal was bustling with activity. Far out there in the river, the Naples based *Irpinia* was already visible to the naked eye. As she got nearer, she appeared whiter and brighter. Discharge waters gushed out of the side openings and ran down the hull of the ship, following the path of rust streaks that went way past the water-line.

The waters of the Saint Lawrence were of an unusual light green color reflecting, perhaps, the sense of anticipation and the restlessness of the crowd that was waiting for the big white steamship to dock and discharge its human cargo: workers, peasants, abandoned wives about to rejoin their husbands, children about to join their parents, parents about to rejoin their children. Their sense of anticipation gave rise, inevitably, to restlessness and worry.

Among the crowd there was Fred, in his forties, with reddish blond hair and light blue eyes. Leaning on a wall, he too was anxiously waiting for the *Irpinia* to dock. With one hand he held a pipe to his mouth, with the other he seemed to be holding something in the pocket of his English style, off-white trench coat. He kept looking around, studying the crowd with a sense of apathy. Then, as if tired of leaning against the wall, he started to move. He walked with an aristocratic gait in a staccato fashion, so much so, in fact, that many turned to look at him and turned back to make comments.

The ship docked, the gangway was lowered into place and some officials quickly climbed aboard. Soon after, the passengers began descending the gangway. They made their way through the crowd of shouting porters and formed a line in front of the tables where the Canadian authorities sat.

The waiting crowd was no longer silent. Their anxiety, their restlessness had turned into impatience. Names were being called out and dialects mingled creating one great confusion. Outstretched arms waved greetings that often went unanswered.

Fred had come forward and had pulled his hand out of his pocket. In it, he held a photograph. He looked at it over and over again, as if he were afraid he might not recognize the person he was waiting for.

He saw a young man just over twenty years of age but as self-assured in demeanor as a mature person. He understood that this was his man. He followed him with his eyes, then gave a signal in the direction of the crowd. Two rough looking characters rushed toward the young man.

"Roberto Perussi?" Fred shouted.

Meanwhile, the two rough looking characters had unceremoniously taken possession of the young man's luggage.

"Roberto Perussi?" Fred asked again, taking the young man by the arm and leading him towards the exit.

"Yes, I am Roberto Perussi," the youngster answered, trying to free himself. "What do you want?"

"My name is Fred Bonfanti. No time to explain just now, but please, follow me."

Roberto hesitated. He didn't know what to say, nor what to do. He would have liked to resist, but then he noticed that two other types were heading their way. He had no choice but let himself be escorted to the exit by the man in the trench coat.

He had expected to be met by his uncles. Instead, he found himself confronted by a stranger who was ordering him around, while two individuals had taken his luggage and two others were following him a short distance away. He felt drained out of all energies and didn't have the strength, or the will, to fight back.

He was pushed in the front seat of a black Oldsmobile, and didn't know what else to do but relax and pull out a cigarette. He had hardly tried to look for matches when a soft hand appeared from behind and flicked on a cigarette lighter.

As the car was speeding through the streets of the city, Roberto pretended to look around so as not to speak or ask the questions that were burning in his chest.

The Oldsmobile came to a stop in front of a bungalow-style house. Before Roberto had a chance to reach for the door handle, the door was opened for him and Fred motioned for him to get out.

Roberto stepped out, turned around and noticed that the individuals who had opened the door for him were checking him out from head to toe, no smiles, impassive like marble statues. He started to walk toward the house. The front door was opened from the inside, as if someone had been there waiting for his arrival. He turned to look at Fred, who motioned to him to get in.

They walked through a long corridor, then down two flights of marble stairs. Another door opened up at the bottom of the staircase and they entered a huge, elegantly furnished room. At the far end there was a semicircular bar. One wall was covered with shelves stuffed with elegantly bound books and a large desk surrounded by soft chairs stood in one corner of the room. Roberto drew a sigh of relief when he noticed that his suitcases had been deposited next to the desk.

"Uncle Nick and Uncle John could not be here to meet you," Fred told him.

He pretended not to hear and looked around, as if searching for something. Then Fred planted himself in front of him and he could no longer avoid him.

"This will be your house, Roberto," Fred told him. "Mine too, for a while at least. Here are the keys, the smaller one is for the front door, the larger for the gate."

Roberto was flabbergasted and didn't take the keys. After all, the man was a total stranger. And this stranger, who insisted on giving him a set of house keys, was beginning to get on his nerves.

"I beg your pardon?" he said. He carefully studied Fred who seemed to have turned into stone in his off-white trench coat. "I don't even know who you are," he continued, "and I don't think that I like you very much. I cannot stay here one minute longer, and certainly I will not take those keys."

"Listen to me, young man," Fred said, blocking his way. "You just got here, you wouldn't even know where to go and what to do. I advise you to listen to me, and listen carefully. I am your uncles' trustee, their manager in other words. It is imperative that we two become friends and that we address each other on more friendly terms from now on."

"May I ask where my uncles are? You haven't even told me where they are!" Roberto said, with a tone of voice that let it be known that he wasn't buying any of this yet.

"They are not in Montreal. They left three days ago, rather suddenly, for business reasons. Is that any better?"

"Maybe," Roberto said. He followed Fred to the couch, then added: "Tell me, then . . ." he continued. He stopped, as if to apologize for the tone of his voice, then resumed in a friendlier and warmer manner: "Tell me something more about my uncles. Where are they? When will I be able to see them?"

"Unfortunately, Roberto," Fred answered, after a brief pause with which he intended to carefully choose his words, "you won't see your uncles for quite a while. They are not so young any more, you see. Like all people who have worked hard all their lives at a certain age they cease to be in the best of health. The climate here in Montreal, as you will soon find out, is not the best when your health is not outstanding. So, following doctors' orders, they left for better climes."

"Are they all that sick then?" Roberto quickly asked, unable to hide his concern.

Fred lit his pipe and went to the bar to fix himself a drink. Roberto followed him with his eyes, anxious to hear the answer to his question.

He was his uncles' only heir. If what they said back home was true, if what his mother used to tell him before she died and if he were to believe what they themselves wrote in their letters, his uncles had amassed quite a fortune.

Roberto had left Italy because he knew all this. He wanted to be near his rich uncles when they died, near his inheritance to take possession of it when the moment came. He knew that had he remained in Italy, lawyers, executors and the law of both countries would have meddled and his uncles' fortune, hard earned for sure, would have gone up in smoke before reaching him.

"No," Fred answered, once he got back to his seat. "They aren't really all that sick. Nonetheless, they have to take care of themselves so as not to get really all that sick."

Roberto Perussi had trouble understanding. If they weren't all that sick, shouldn't they have waited for him to arrive before going away? Surely they could have waited. They could have left together for wherever it was they had to go. He could even have been of help to them, away from home. If nothing else, he could have been good company to them. They themselves had often written that they felt lonely, they missed family affection and they very much felt the loss of his mother, their only sister.

"When will they be back?" he asked.

"I don't really know for sure. I suppose the doctor will decide when it's time. If it should happen that they cannot come back, we will go join them. But why not leave all this alone now and go out to dinner? It's about time, and maybe I can introduce you to a few people worthwhile knowing."

"Okay, let's go," Roberto agreed, while getting up. "I am not really hungry, but I feel a need to stretch my legs."

"I am sure you do. After fifteen days out at sea, eh?"

"Yeah, fifteen days," Roberto confirmed. Then he added, somewhat gleefully: "But I spent them well. There was this girl, traveling alone. Nice looking girl, coming here to marry a man she has never met, only seen him in pictures. He wanted an Italian wife, she wanted to come to Canada!"

"You went to bed with her?"

"Well, why not!" Roberto said, as if begging the other's pardon. "She used to get sea sick in her cabin and was afraid to sleep alone, so she stayed with me. What a girl! The man who's marrying her is a lucky bastard! She gave me her address and told me I could visit her, during the day, whenever I wanted."

"Let me tell you something straight off, Roberto," Fred interrupted. "Those women are best left alone. Don't bother with them. You'll always have plenty of ladies around here. You'll have so many that you'll be forced to turn them away. Just wait, and after you get the hang of things, you'll see, there won't be any time left for you to get bored."

They arrived on Stanley Street. The kind of people that crowded the street reminded him of Piazza Colonna and Piazza del Popolo and via Margutta, Via del Babuino, the Termini Station. It seemed to him as if bits of Rome had flown there just to give the street that particular feeling. There were restaurants and cafés and in front of these, beatniks milled around passing the time. Once in a while one of them would greet Fred with a knowing smile, a motion of the head, a gesture of friendship.

"Come on, let's go in," Fred said, when they arrived at a restaurant. The sign at the entrance read *Carmen*. "The owner is a Jewish lady who got away from the Nazis. She bought this restaurant with Nazi money. Look at the crowd," he said with disgust, as they walked in. "It's always like this. These Jews are sure lucky!"

"These Jews?" Roberto underscored the words. "You say it as if it were a sin to be born a Jew."

"Sit down, Roberto. Sit down," he then added. "Maybe you are right. It isn't a sin to be born a Jew. Jesus himself was born a Jew. He was no sinner. Yet we caused him to die on the cross, didn't we?"

A waitress, smiling with familiarity, approached Fred who smiled back, then stretched his hand as if to touch her. The girl swerved to avoid him and looked around. Roberto knew that Fred had done it to impress him but said nothing.

"How is *signora* Carmen today?" Fred asked.

"The *signora* is just fine," the waitress answered, somewhat annoyed. "What will it be?"

"Dinner has been ordered," Fred said, with a wink. "Just tell the Chef that Fred Bonfanti is here. By the way, bring a bottle of Dom Perignon, best vintage."

"You know that we are not allowed to serve wine and liquors, Mr. Bonfanti," the girl pointed out.

"Never mind. You know what we want and you know where to get it, don't you?" Fred answered. The girl nodded and went away. "No beer and no wine in this kind of place, dear boy. To sell alcoholic beverages, you need a special license from the Canadian Liquor Board. You can get it either by paying top dollars or by having the right connections. Your uncles, for instance, could get any license they wanted: for themselves or for others."

"About my uncles," Roberto picked up the subject again. "What is it that they do? I mean, what line of work? In their letters they never said much about work. We knew that they were doing well, that they made lots of money. But that's just about it."

"Your uncles are gods here, Roberto. They know how to pluck money out of thin air," Fred answered laughing, and making grabbing gestures with one hand as if he were really plucking money out of thin air.

Roberto Perussi was ecstatic, even though he hadn't learned anything new about his uncles from Fred's answers. It was perhaps really true that Canada was an extraordinary land, a land full of surprises where everything was possible, even fishing money out of thin air, as Fred had said. He was up on cloud nine and felt a great need to show off, to begin his new life.

"*Bonsoir, mes amis, bonsoir,*" he heard a voice whisper. His head was still up in the clouds.

He turned and was confronted by a rather plump individual a few years older than him. He wore a brown velvet suit that made him look even fatter. He leaned on the table resting his weight on his hands, a peculiar smile on his face, his bulging round eyes alternately staring at Fred and at Roberto.

"Who is this guy anyway?" Roberto asked.

"This guy is an Italian too," the plump fellow answered. "And his name is Pierino di Nunno. Pleased to meet you," he replied, while extending his hand. "Who might you be, may I ask?"

Roberto didn't answer. He looked questioningly at Fred who just smiled, amused.

"This is Roberto Perussi," Fred then said. "Be kind to Pierino, Roberto, and you too will soon become Montreal's beloved child."

"Roberto. Roberto," Pierino repeated the name to himself. "It's a name that I don't like much. I am going to cut it in two, Ro and Berto. Berto is rather ugly, isn't it? It reminds me of the Bertha from fairy tales who spent all her time at the spinning wheel. Ro, on the other hand, is short and meaningless, it doesn't excite me much. I'll put the name together again, break it down differently and, *voilà*, out comes Rob, an Americanized name that pleases me very much. Pleased to meet you, Rob."

"Don't pay any attention to him, Roberto," Fred laughed. "That's how he is. Deep down, though, he is a nice guy, everyone loves him. Isn't that so, Pierino?"

"If you say so, it must be true. But I wouldn't know, would I?" Pierino answered. "Anyway, you should stop being egotistical and paranoid and let others live as they please. You too shortened your name when you came here, didn't you? From a common Federico Barbarossa you have become an important Fred Copperbeard or, more befitting perhaps, Fred Goldbeard? Now then, stop addressing our friend here with that ugly bourgeois name and call him Rob. Otherwise we won't be friends anymore."

"Okay, Pierino. You are the boss around here, and since you are boss, I take my hat off to you!"

"A filthy capitalist like yourself might be a boss, not me. You see, I never have any money in my pockets, whereas bosses, everyone knows, have pockets bulging with money. I am a poor, penniless communist mistakenly born in a small nowhere town in Italy and transplanted here by a banal and unfathomable mistake."

Pushing a cart, the waitress approached the table. She gave Pierino a relaxed, friendly smile, calmly proceeded to set the table for three, then started serving the food.

"Voici ma maîtresse," Pierino said, looking at her in admiration. Since the girl appeared to be irritated, he added: *"Ma maîtresse d'ecole,"* that is! You know that I love you, my dear, don't you?"

"You'll never change, Pierino," the girl said, shaking her head and smiling. *"Tu seras toujours un enfant."*

"Oui, l'enfant du bon Dieu, mon amour," Pierino added, as the girl walked away.

"Quite a character this Pierino, isn't he?" Roberto told Fred, but his intended listener was really Pierino himself.

"Quite a character, quite a character," Pierino answered quickly. "But what does this word *character* really mean? *Je ne le connais pas.* Did you know that last night she had the gall to ask me to go to bed with her? She actually wanted to go to bed with me!"

"Don't pay any attention to him, Roberto. He is just trying to impress you," Fred said.

"Quite funny," Pierino said, trying to defend himself. "How much you want to bet that tonight I'll take her to bed?"

"You need money, don't you, Pierino?" Fred asked.

"You know very well that Pierino never needs any money," Pierino answered disdainfully. "You also know that Pierino always has money in his pockets even though he is always broke. So there you go, yes: if you lend me fifty bucks, in exactly one week you'll get your filthy money back."

Fred pulled out a roll of bills. He counted off fifty dollars to Pierino who quickly grabbed the bills and shoved them in the breast pocket of his jacket, as if afraid that Fred might withdraw the hand that was offering the bills.

"You dare call others boss? You'll get it back in exactly one week without interest of course," Pierino said.

"Yes, I know, without interest," Fred confirmed. He then took some more money and, without counting, gave it to Roberto. "You probably have *lire* on you, don't you? Here, you'll need it. I'll leave you with Pierino now, I have an errand to run. Have fun. I'll see you later at home, Pierino will take you. Tomorrow we'll go buy you a car, you'll need one. Won't he, Pierino?"

"A car is a dream for poor bastards like me, but is a necessity for bosses. If Rob needs a car, it is because he is a boss too. I never liked bosses, I want you to know that. You guys are the only filthy exception."

"If you don't stop it, one nice day Fred might bust your pretty face. What do you say?"

"I say you are an ill-bred bully, but you'll never be able to put your filthy hands on Pierino's pretty face."

"That's enough, I am going now," Fred said. "So I'll see you later at home, right, Roberto?"

"You mean, 'right, Rob?'" Pierino repeated his words as if to correct him, forcing him to shorten Roberto's name. "If you say Rob, you'll see him at home tonight. Otherwise you will see neither Rob nor Berto, because I'll make him sleep with one of my lady friends."

"Listen, Fred," Roberto said, amused, happy to have made a new friend. "Let's make Pierino happy, shall we? Rob suits me just fine. Fred, Nick, John . . . Why not Rob?"

"Okay, Mister Rob," Fred said, finally. "See you later then."

"Till later," Roberto answered.

"Who are Nick and John, may I ask?" Pierino asked him, after Fred left.

"Curtesi. Nick and John Curtesi, my mother's brothers," Roberto replied. "Do you know them?"

"Sure do!" Pierino answered. "Who doesn't know them? I have never actually met them, but I know of them. So you are their nephew, eh?"

"Yeah," Roberto confirmed.

His tone bespoke an apology. He meant to say that he was their nephew not because he deserved to be, but because that was how things were.

"Then you too are a big shot. I suppose I should feel important tonight?"

Roberto felt like a different person, like he had always been a big shot. Even though he wasn't born a big shot, he knew that it had always been his fate to become one some day. He had to boast. He wanted others to know, he wanted Pierino to know that he really was a big shot, but he didn't quite know what to say.

"Where shall we go?"

It was the most he could manage to say. He leaned back on the chair, turned his head slightly toward Pierino and rested his open hands on the table. He did this in order to assume what he considered an important, bossy-like pose.

"How much did stingy Fred give you?" Pierino asked.

Rob pulled out his money, but before he had time to count it Pierino got a hold of it and started counting it himself.

"Two hundred and forty dollars!" he exclaimed. "Not so stingy, after all! I don't think I ever had two hundred and forty dollars in my hands all at once. We could go all the way to heaven and then come back with two hundred and forty dollars. But heaven doesn't exist, nor do purgatory and hell. These things were invented by priests for children and other innocent creatures, like the most divine Alighieri. Keep your two hundred and forty dollars, you might need them for other things. Pierino will take you to explore his own paradise, where there are no priests to collect the cover charge. You'll only need money to buy a cup of coffee, or a cup of hot chocolate at the most. What do you say?"

"I say that I already like your paradise very much, Pierino. Shall we go then?"

"Let's go!"

They walked up Stanley Street, then moved on to Sherbrooke without saying a word. Roberto kept on looking around. Pierino walked next to him and he too, head high, looked around. Once in a while he would look at Roberto as if he were trying to read his thoughts, or as if he were waiting for him to ask questions.

"This is McGill University. English," Pierino said, breaking the silence. "There is another important university, l'Université de Montréal. French. There, on the hill behind us. You can't see it but it's there. A little more to go and we will be there."

"Where's it we are going, Pierino?" Roberto asked.

"To a place called La Paloma. It's not like Carmen. Carmen is for money-people. That's why you'll never find there the kind of atmosphere suited for people like us, young people I mean, people like you and me. You'll see, you'll see. Further down there is another spot, El Cortijo. The best café in town."

They got to La Paloma. They went up a flight of stairs, crossed a hallway, went down another flight of stairs and emerged into a large, musty room. Some people with long beards and long hair were playing chess. Other strange looking characters were talking in whispers, as if plotting something. There were also some beautiful girls around.

"Let's go to that table," Pierino said, pointing to a table where a couple was sitting, one guy all wrapped up in an old duffle coat and a girl with long blond hair and a rosy but light, almost transparent complexion.

"*Qu'est que tu fais ici, avec mon ennemi, ma chérie?*" Pierino asked the girl, while kissing her on the cheek. "You are my friend, and I don't like it when you speak to the enemy."

"Yes, Pierino," the girl said, amused. "I am your friend but I talk to whoever I please, you know that. I don't care if you have enemies. Your friends are my friends and so are your enemies."

"*Bon Dieu!*" Pierino exclaimed. "There shall never be truce between me and women! Line, Tony, this is a new friend of mine, Rob Perussi." Then, referring to Tony, he said to Rob: "This guy here, Rob, is a poor liberal revolutionary who will never amount to anything. He came all the way from Italy to declare the independence of Quebec."

"Stop fooling around and sit down," Tony said. "You too, Rob, please sit down. I'm pleased to meet you."

"Thank you," Rob said, as he sat down. "A pleasure to meet you both," he added, and shook hands with both Tony and Line.

"In a week there will be elections," Tony said. "I was just talking to Line about it. There is a lot of work to be done and a lot of money to be made. Are you up to it, Pierino? We could ask your friend to help too, of course. What do you both say?"

"Well, I just arrived this afternoon from Italy. . ."

"You actually just came from Italy?" Line asked, with great interest. When she saw Rob nod affirmatively, she added: "How wonderful. I dream about Italy! I dream about it night and day. Where do you come from? I mean, where in Italy?"

"I'm from Rome."

"Rome!" the girl sighed. She slumped in ecstasy against the back of the chair. "Why on earth did you leave Rome to come to this monstrous city, Rob? Why did you do it?" she added reproachfully.

"Because if he hadn't," Pierino replied, "he wouldn't have met me and now you, nor would he have met our Quebecois friend Tony, here."

"Stop this foolish nonsense," Tony said. "Let's be serious and go back to the election: can I count you in?"

"It all depends on what we have to do," Pierino said. "You know that I don't like to work. Work is humiliating, so any kind of work is out. What is this all about?"

"All you have to do is vote. That's all, really. The more you vote, the more you get paid."

"I cannot vote," Rob said. "I am an Italian citizen."

"Don't you worry about that, Rob," Tony said. "Everybody can vote here, Canadians and non Canadians alike, the rich and the poor, the living and the dead."

"In that case . . ." Rob said.

"In that case . . ." Pierino echoed.

3

Election day was nearing. Rob was so excited at the prospect of making some money of his own that he could hardly wait. He had said nothing to Fred, he didn't think it was necessary. Besides, if he earned some money, he would be that much better off. Not that he needed any, but the idea of earning some really excited him.

Fred had bought him a shiny new Ford and kept on giving him money without even asking if he needed any. Such must have been the instructions he had received from his uncles, Rob thought. If that was true, it also had to be true that his uncles were rich, filthy rich.

A new life had begun for him and he was more than ready to live it. It was the kind of life he had always dreamed of. A life with no worries but plenty of money in his pockets, money he had not earned by the sweat of his brow, therefore that much easier to spend as he wished.

Tony informed them that they would be working for a party called Civic Action League whose principal exponent, the incumbent Executive Commissioner, was also Italian. His opponent, an old gentleman named Lomascolo, was running very strong against him.

Lomascolo, a Sicilian, boasted having on his side not only most of his fellow Sicilians, a rather numerous lot, but also most of the early, and a good part of the later wave of immigrants because he was endorsed by one of the leading Italian papers published in Montreal. Gagliano, the incumbent Commissioner, had been savagely attacked in the paper's editorials. While these attacks were considered worrisome revelations by some, by others they were severely criticized.

"One shouldn't air one's dirty linens in public. Nor should they be given to dogs to drag around in the streets," some people said.

This was of no interest to Rob. He couldn't care less whether Gagliano would be put back into office or not. The only reason he had accepted to work in the elections was to have something exciting to do and earn some money.

On election day, Pierino and a driver passed by Rob's house to pick him up and go to one of the dispatch offices, as Tony Ruti had told them. Rob and Pierino had been assigned to the North section of town, District Number Ten, where the Italian population was thickest.

"I haven't slept much in two nights," the driver said, a French Canadian who spoke an incomprehensible brand of *joual*. "Election time is always like this: a thankless job. But it pays well."

"You know much about these things, don't you?" Pierino asked.

"Sure do. I worked for these people two years ago too. Running here and there, taking people first to one ward, then another, then again to another, and so on. I took the same people to vote all over the city I don't know how many times, dozens of times maybe."

"This can't be legal?" Rob asked, worried.

"Legal? Come now, nothing is legal here," Pierino said. "But we do everything just the same and with great efficiency."

"What about the police?" Rob asked again.

"They mind their own business. We aren't much worried about them," the driver said. "They know and they play along. Besides, they don't want to lose their jobs, do they? Catch my drift?"

"It's all a joke, then, isn't it?" Rob commented. "A big, ugly joke!"

"Not quite," the driver said. "Let's say that it is a game of convenience and cleverness. The most clever wins. In the provincial elections, two years ago, they screwed us. Our opposition was much more clever than us. They even managed to get the police on their side. I myself was well aware of it."

"And what made you suspect it?" Pierino asked.

"As I said, I have experience. It's a question of intuition."

"So what should the Union have done then?" Pierino asked.

"They should have resigned themselves to losing. They should have given up power without a fight and with a smile, so to speak. Their game was getting old anyway, it smelled pretty stale. Once in a while people are entitled to something new."

"These 'people' would be the unhappy ones, I suppose?" Rob insinuated.

"Those who feel the need to put their hands on the bounty of power," the driver continued. "Political commitment is the prerogative of a small circle of people. Those who find themselves barred from it react by instigating public opinion. At the next election, all that's left to do is watch the pieces fall into place."

"What are your thoughts on the current elections?" Pierino asked.

"I shouldn't, but I'll say my piece anyway. Our side has grabbed as much as it can. I don't see the results of this election coming our way. Most of the police seem to be allied with the other side. Who knows, maybe they too have been figuring things out."

"The police is with the other side?" Rob asked, a bit worried.

"Some of our dispatch holes east and west of the city have been raided. There have been some arrests, the last one just this morning."

"Could it be dangerous for us too?" Rob said, alarmed.

"I don't think so. Not in our district, anyway," the driver said, shrugging his shoulders. Then he added: "Of course, I can't rule it out either!"

By now they had gotten to the corner of Saint Dominique and Dante Streets. They parked the car and walked the rest of the way to a cellar across from the Church Madonna della Difesa.

The place was owned by a man called Nino Crudele, a pioneer of Italian immigration, a fascist to the bone. Soon after his arrival, he had become a wealthy man by slowly working his way up in the select circle of bosses in the newly forming Italian community. In all fairness, his business had been clean and most honest.

He opened an inn of sorts and began to take in, free of charge, as many of his fellow Italian immigrants as he could manage to get in touch with: men who left their homes with just the shirt on their back and arrived in droves, thoroughly helpless. When they came off the boats, all they wanted was a bit of help. *Signor* Crudele was always there for them.

He took them in, fed them, found them their first job. He gained their confidence and swayed them into taking residence in his area of business. This soon became the heart of the community, and a gold mine for Nino Crudele who, meantime, had begun buying real estate in the area.

He had patterned himself after the Great Master Mussolini. Like him, he was a dictator of sorts who cherished the memories of a fascist era about which he had only heard others speak. Mussolini had made his heart swell with pride when ten million of his gallant soldiers had made the entire world tremble in fear. This fascination had landed him in concentration camps for several months during the war. Those were pleasant memories: a great heritage to hand down to the future generations who, a full fifteen years later, still shuddered with pride when his band, a fascist pin proudly displayed on their lapel, played Mussolini's hallmark tunes, from Giovinezza to Faccetta Nera, up and down Dante Street.

The three walked down to the basement and gained access to a big room that looked like a military headquarters. City maps studded with multicolored flags were hanging on the walls. Voter registration books for the entire city were piled up high on large folding tables. The men seated around the tables looked hot, tired and sleepy. They must have been up all night making last minute preparations.

A tall and broad fellow sat in one corner, isolated from the others. In all likelihood, he was the revered Nino Crudele. Ruddy complexion, curly and gray-brown hair, hands held over his bulging belly, he cut a figure worthy of his title of *Commendatore*, obtained from the old Italian government when he could say that Mussolini was his friend. He did nothing but watch and listen; occasionally he looked towards the entrance, or through the windows out onto Dante Street.

Sitting on top of one of the tables, oblivious to the papers he was scattering around, was a man in shirt sleeves and suspenders. Under his arm he had a broad leather strap that connected to a holster containing a small revolver. He had all the mannerisms of an outlaw, but could easily have been a policeman.

A thin mustached man in his forties sitting behind one of the desks was, no doubt, Gagliano himself. His Calabrian origins were clearly revealed by the French he spoke as he gave orders to three young drivers who, a moment later, left whispering *"Okay . . . ça marche . . . parfait!"*

When Rob's turn came, the Calabrian motioned to him to come forward. He did, followed by Pierino and the driver.

"Everything is set, as far as the price is concerned?" he asked.

"Yes, it is," Pierino nodded.

"You know what to do, I gather."

"I would like to know," Rob tried to ask.

"Look here," Gagliano interrupted him, as if he had read his mind. "You won't have any trouble, if that's what's bothering you. The police have been paid off to leave you alone. We are well protected, and so are you. You have a driver who knows his business well. All you have to do is vote for this list of candidates and when you put your ballot in the box, you slip in five or six additional ballots that have already been filled out."

"Just a minute!" Roberto objected.

"The polling clerks won't even look at you, don't worry," Gagliano interrupted him again, as if he had the gift of being able to read minds. "They know the names that our people will use from ward to ward."

"Just what are our names?" Pierino asked.

"The driver will give you names at each of the wards, together with the extra ballots," replied a bald man who sounded well educated, and well informed.

"To start with," the Calabrian continued, while rummaging through a pile of papers and notes, "you'll go to two wards not far from here, in district number ten. Polls 87 and 88. Your names will be Giulio Barone and Dom Cousineau."

He handed them a couple of slips of paper and the filled ballots.

"Your name, address and occupation is written down," he added. "You'll have to memorize everything 'cause you may be asked. At polls 113, 114 and 117 your names will be Antonio Martino and John Brodeur. Is that clear?"

"I guess so," Rob said, with a forced smile.

"You'll get an advance at noon, and this evening you'll get the rest of the four hundred dollars."

"Just what are we supposed to use to buy our smokes and snacks from now till noon?" Pierino remarked.

"Alright, you drive a hard bargain. Here are fifty dollars. You'll get another fifty at noon, the rest in the evening. Is that okay?"

"That's better," Pierino confirmed.

They picked up their money and left. The driver, who hadn't said a word the whole time, followed them.

They were in a constant rush, from one ward to another, from one nest of dispatches to another. In the afternoon, they heard on the car radio that some of the dispatches had been arrested on the west side. Rob and Pierino looked each other in the eyes, each hoping the other would give a sign as to what to do.

"The west side is not protected," the driver said. "We are lucky we aren't working there at all. Bail will be quickly posted for them, and they will be released before nightfall with lots of apologies, I am sure. The League always pays, they don't want to risk having their people questioned. The same thing happened during the provincial elections."

"Maybe it's like you say," Rob said. "But I don't want to be caught. We have done most of the work and have received only a small part of the money. I don't want anything more to do with this."

They had arrived in front of Polls 87, 93, 94. The driver stopped the car and opened the back door by means of an ingenious contraption hooked up to the back rest of his seat.

"As you wish," he said. "But I do have to let them know. I can't do less than that now, can I?"

"Okay, tell them that we got scared by the news we heard on the radio," Pierino said nonchalantly.

"Please, give them our best," Rob added.

They got out, moved away and hailed a cab. When they got to Rob's house, they breathed a sigh of relief and opened a bottle of beer.

"To Gagliano," Rob toasted, raising the bottle in the air, then to his mouth.

At that very moment the door bell rang. Rob looked at Pierino questioningly and went to the door. He was confronted by the same guy he had seen in the Dante Street office, the one with the gun under his arm. The driver and a rather brawny character were also there.

"We're well organized, don't you think?" the guy with the gun said. "You needn't be afraid, everything has been perfectly well organized. I could have picked you up in front of the polling place, but I wanted to show you how efficient we are in our line of work."

"Who is it?" Pierino asked from the kitchen, when he heard voices at the door.

"Friends," the other guy yelled out.

When Pierino walked in the living room and saw the driver and the other two men, he didn't act surprised. He had expected them all along.

"Good afternoon," the gangster, or policeman said, whichever he was. "Do you mind following us back to work?"

Rob tried to object. Pierino pretended to look for something in his pockets.

"You do want to stay healthy, don't you? You see, so far no one has given us any trouble and we're just itching to exercise our knuckles a bit."

Rob didn't say another word. He knew that they weren't kidding. He picked up his jacket from the couch and motioned to the others to step outside before him.

"No, no. After you," the guy said, forcing a smile.

Rob and Pierino walked out, followed by the three guys. The one with the gun walked out last and checked the door to make sure it was properly closed.

They picked up their rounds from polls 87, 93 and 94 where they had left. By five in the afternoon they had voted in almost every ward of Montreal North and were taken back to the cellar on Dante Street to collect their three hundred dollars. They found other dispatches there, waiting to be paid. They all looked relieved and satisfied.

The two thugs who had come to fetch them at home were leaning against the wall behind Gagliano. They stood, arms crossed and motionless, like stone statues. There was a big and fat fellow among the dispatches. Rob was certain he had seen his picture on leaflets or in newspaper ads. He took a better look at him, and recognized the big, fat Italian who was often featured at the *soirées de lutte* at Faillon Stadium. For sure, he thought, most of these people were well known by the courts and at police stations throughout the city. One could tell from their attitude, from the look on their faces, from the arrogance they showed as they picked the money and left without saying a word.

"There you are," the Calabrian muttered as Rob and Pierino approached. "Everything went well after all, didn't it?"

"With a bit of luck, yes," Rob lied, hoping that the man hadn't found out that he and Pierino had tried to weasel out of the deal.

"Well, we should thank our organization too, shouldn't we? Shouldn't we, Pierino?"

"Of course," Pierino answered with a smile.

"You think you might be interested in earning another hundred dollars each? I understand you worked efficiently and fast. Except for that justifiable and forgivable incident, of course."

"We couldn't possibly keep on doing this work," Pierino ventured to say. "We have already voted in all the wards!"

"If we go back, we risk being recognized," Roberto added.

"I didn't have the same job in mind," Gagliano said, winking. "We'll put you outside of two different wards. Most of the Italians who are on their way home from work will be voting there. You would be doing them a favor by showing them how to vote while slipping them a few bucks."

"Too risky," Rob said, lowering his head. "Besides, since we didn't know we had to work late, we have made arrangements with some girls who are now waiting for us. We wanted to, you know, celebrate your victory."

"Good, good," the Calabrian man said. "If all goes well, if I am voted back into office, I'll have another job for you. But we will talk about that another time."

"What kind of job would that be?" Rob asked, anxious once more.

"Let's not talk about it now. In due time, Tony Ruti will let you know."

Rob and Pierino went to Carmen's to celebrate. They were very happy with their day's earnings, especially Pierino who had never seen so much money in his life.

He had already thought of a thousand ways to spend it. He wanted to go to New York and spend some time in the Greenwich Village. He wanted to send for a Cossack hat in Russia or a pair of boots in Texas. He would have loved to go to Paris and Rome, but knew that his money would be barely sufficient for a one way ticket.

While they were eating, Fred came in. He sat with them and ordered something for himself.

"I haven't seen you all day. Where the hell have you been?" he asked.

"Oh, we went strolling up and down the city," Pierino said.

"With what? Rob's car has been parked in front of the house all day long," Fred remarked.

"We took another car," Roberto said, smiling. "And a uniformed chauffeur just for us."

"What do you think of that, eh?" Pierino chided. "You see, we are becoming big shots too."

He pulled out the roll of bills he had gotten from Gagliano.

"This," he said, "is one day's worth of work."

"What kind of work?" Fred asked suspiciously and with a tone of reproach.

"Election work," Rob said, in a whisper and innocently laughing.

"Telegraphist!" Pierino added.

"You didn't even tell me? May I at least ask: whom did you work for?"

"The Calabrian," Pierino was quick to point out.

"You should have said something to me," Fred commented. "His re-election and the overall success of his plan, now that the brothers aren't here, depend entirely on me, and he darn well knows it. You should have said something to me, I would have given you an easier job and you would have made twice as much money."

"You see," Pierino said, "you really are a big stinker. You had the chicken that lays the golden eggs, and you don't tell us."

"I did say that I looked for you all day long, didn't I?"

"Granted. But you could have said something yesterday, or the day before. Why didn't you?"

"Okay, okay. You're always right, Pierino. No one can argue with you. How much did you get?"

"Four hundred," Roberto answered. "Four hundred each, that is."

"Well, you could have earned much more. In any event, there will be more to be made once Gagliano gets back into office, I guarantee you that. But we'll talk about that when the time comes."

"That's what Gagliano said too. May we know what this is all about?" Roberto asked.

"We'll talk about it when I come back. I am leaving for Mexico in the morning."

"Mexico?" Roberto asked. "And what for?"

"Uncle Nick. He phoned me last night and asked me to go to Mexico in order to formalize agreements with some of our agents there."

"What agents?" Rob asked, still hoping to find out something about his uncles' business.

"Business agents, of course," Fred answered, quickly. "They ship us merchandise that we sell wholesale here in Canada. To be more precise, we don't even see the merchandise. We draw up a contract, money is exchanged, and in a matter of twenty four hours we make enormous sums of money."

Fred said nothing else. He finished eating, paid the bill for everyone and excused himself, saying that he had to see some people before leaving for Mexico.

4

Things were going very well in Roberto's new life. At first he was sorry that he didn't hear from his uncles, then he stopped asking about them. His business was now with Fred, he had plenty of money and lived in style. With Fred's help and advice, he managed to keep risk at a healthy distance and except for once or twice, he never had any troubles to speak of.

One day, however, the newspapers carried headlines about his uncle Nick's arrest. While waiting for trial, he was being detained in the high security jail of Bordeaux. His brother John had been able to take cover abroad.

Fred and Rob tried to connect with those who, before Rob's arrival from Italy, had been ordered by the brothers to disperse around the world in a precise and prescribed manner. In light of the latest developments, it was necessary to make sure that they all had the same story to tell.

Things precipitated fast. Since drugs were found on Nick Curtesi while he was in jail, he was extradited to Toronto and some of the old gang were picked up by the police. They were able to prove that they were upstanding Canadian citizens and that they knew nothing about Nick Curtesi's drugs and were released. Fred and Rob were also stopped for routine questioning, then quickly released. As usual, the police were grasping at straws. The investigation was soon abandoned and all returned to normal.

A few weeks later, between Saint Laurent and Saint Denis, near a Sicilian restaurant not far from Chinatown, a night club dancer was killed, shot from a speeding car.

The usual investigation was launched, and one day after Rob was arrested again. He was able to provide the police with an air-tight alibi and was released on five hundred dollars bail.

He knew then that he could no longer go quite so freely about his business. He knew that from now on, he had to look over his shoulder every step of the way. These thoughts began to trouble him a great deal, but there was nothing he could do about it.

One morning, shortly after the Chinatown incident, two policemen came to his house. They found him in bed with some girl, a dancer that he had rescued from the claws of a pimp.

"What do you want?" he asked, when he opened the door and saw the two men in uniform.

"Get dressed. You are coming with us," one of them said.

"Listen, I don't much like the idea of always having you underfoot," he protested. "I'm clean, and you know it. Ask the young lady, if you don't believe me," he added, pointing to the girl who, by then, had put some clothes on and had come to the door.

"Now, that's a novel approach. We should ask the woman with whom you sleep to vouch for you?" the policeman snickered. "Too convenient, I'd say. Let's go, come on. We do not have all day."

"But we haven't done anything," the girl protested. "You don't have the right to pick us up like this."

"Your friend here is out on bail," the other policeman said, with a sarcastic smile. "He is obliged to come with us whenever we want."

"In any event, we just want to ask him a few questions," the other policeman added. "Why are you making such a fuss over nothing? We need to shed some light on a recent murder, and on prostitution in general here in Montreal. It is strictly in your own interest, young lady," he then added.

"Like hell it is," the girl said angrily, as she struggled to put on the stockings that she had been carrying slung over her shoulders when she first came to the door. "Aren't you tired of following false leads all the time?"

"Those too can prove useful in flushing out evidence and names," the policeman answered quickly.

"Of course," Rob said. "Meanwhile, you bother us innocent people who mind our own business."

"By the way, what's your line of business, Mr. Perussi?" one of the policemen asked Rob, rather gruffly.

"I work. In summertime I work up north, in Labrador. Besides, I have also worked right here in the city. I have worked for a company."

"If I am not mistaken, you have worked for a real estate organization, haven't you?" the policeman interrupted.

"What's that got to do with it?" Rob replied defensively. "That was a scam and the moment I realized it, I quit. They even owed me some money."

"Just how much exactly did they owe you?" asked the policeman who had questioned him last. He made it quite obvious that his question was meant to insinuate that he knew a lot more about the matter than Rob figured.

"How much?" Rob repeated, nervous. He fumbled with his necktie, trying to make a knot, but he was only succeeding in wrinkling the fabric. "If you don't believe me, I can show you proof."

"Real solid proof, I'm sure! I imagine it's the same kind of proof everyone else has been producing, isn't it so?"

"No. Real proof, I mean. Because I have always been legit. Let me say it again: I can prove it."

"If you don't believe him, I'll vouch for him, as would many others," the girl, Pierrette, said. To appear convincing, she flashed one of her prettiest smiles.

"Yes, you could, I am sure," the policeman answered, while his colleague took upon himself the task to ransack the chest of drawers, a task he seemed to relish a great deal. "You could, but you sleep with him so no one would believe you, would they?"

"Why, is it a crime to go to bed and make love to whomever you please? You see, I happen not to like you but if I did . . ." she smiled engagingly, but she had little effect on the man.

"Shall we go?" he said.

"Sure. Why don't we go?" Rob said, making his way to the door. "Let's get this over with before you start looking in my slippers too."

"You know, I hadn't thought about that," the one who had been rummaging through the chest of drawers said. "Slippers are an excellent hiding place even for drugs."

He picked up one of the slippers, pried the sole loose with a knife and then pealed it all the way back before throwing it on the floor.

"Don't tell me you guys can actually recognize drugs when you see them?" Pierrette said contemptuously.

"Why should we not be able to?"

"Personally, you see, I wouldn't be able to tell drugs apart from dust," Pierrette said, shrugging her shoulders. "That should tell you how much I know about these things. Is it possible that you can't tell by looking at us in the face, in our eyes, that we're not people who use drugs?"

"We see that you're not people who use drugs," the policeman who had remained silent said. "We can also tell that the two of you aren't stupid. Uncle Nick wasn't either, was he Mr. Perussi? You don't take drugs. Of course not! But you do induce others, so you can make money off of them, wouldn't you?"

"But it's a crime, why would we do that?" Rob said, while slamming the door.

"A crime indeed," the policeman exclaimed. "You say it as if you and your kind could tell the difference between crime and charity."

"I think that's enough!" Pierrette lashed back. "If you go on like this, we'll be forced to sue you for defamation."

Sitting in the waiting room at the police station, there was a collection of unsavory characters at that time of night. There were also a few women, hookers by their looks. All were waiting to be questioned. The arrival of Pierrette made a couple of the women stir. They were quickly whisked away to another room, and everything went back to normal.

The questioning sessions didn't last long. Soon it was Pierrette's and Rob's turn and they were introduced to the inspector's office.

"Well, we already know each other, don't we, Pierrette La Fontaine?" the police inspector said.

"I doubt it," Pierrette answered with contempt.

"What about this mug shot then?"

"All that shows," Pierrette said, lowering her head in shame, "is how I was forced to live by a certain person who was . . . who was exploiting me."

"You mean, your pimp!"

"You have no right! He exploited me and you know it," Pierrette yelled. "He threatened to kill me and he beat me up. You guys didn't exactly protect me then, did you? Here, take a look!" she said, uncovering her shoulder and showing the inspector a long scar. "He did this to me with a leather belt."

"You poor thing," the inspector said. Then he added, after a long sigh: "He wasn't too lucky either. He was found dead in the Laurentides in a room at the Motel du Lac. But why am I telling you this when you already know?"

"I read it in the papers," Pierrette answered.

"Of course you did!" the inspector retorted. He put Pierrette's mug shot away and turned to Rob. "And you, Roberto Perussi . . . Your name isn't exactly new in our files either, is it? I would venture to say we are old friends by now."

"If you are referring to the time I was arrested and released on bail."

"No, no. There is much more than that, here," the inspector cut him short. "That whole affair about the land, for instance. But you managed to get out of that, didn't you?"

"I . . ." Rob tried to defend himself, but once again he was cut short by the inspector.

"Of course, you didn't know anything about that, you just furnished the buyers. I know, I know. It was the other guy, the engineer who promised work to those poor unsuspecting countrymen of yours. The engineer was the one who threatened the prospective employers if they didn't hire. It was also he who pocketed the money received from the sale of the worthless land. When those workers were laid off, he didn't have the guts to make good on his threats because he knew that we had the construction sites under surveillance. Of course you, Roberto Perussi, you didn't know anything about all this, did you?"

"Just what are you insinuating?" Rob interrupted.

"Nothing at all, of course," the inspector answered quickly. "However, if the engineer had not ended up in the canal, at Lascine, in your own car, he might have been able to tell us a thing or two, don't you think?"

"Come on now, he was drunk and you know it. I lent him my car the day before the accident, his was in the shop. Don't make unfounded accusations," Rob concluded.

"Yes, he got drunk on water as we know. The autopsy confirmed that. But let's leave it alone for now. It's an old story, even for us. Why don't you tell me something about this girl who was killed in Chinatown?"

"How would we know anything about that?" Rob answered. "The young lady and I are clean."

"Yeah, I already said that you are. But if you care about staying clean, you come see me as soon as you come to know something . . . I am always here, at your disposal. You can go now but be warned: if you don't come looking for us, we'll have to come looking for you."

"What could we possibly know?" Pierrette said.

"One never knows, in our line of work. Sometimes the wind, or maybe ghosts," the inspector smiled, somewhere between kindness and sarcasm. "Till next time, then?"

Time went by. No one said anything more about the girl killed in Chinatown, and Rob and Pierrette were never called back by the police. Indeed, it seemed that this investigation too had been abandoned.

5

One day, while standing across from The Place on Stanley Street, Rob heard the notes of a familiar piano music. There was no doubt in his mind: it was Jack Jackson. Had the black piano player dared to come back in town? Rob remembered quite clearly how Jackson had threatened him before leaving. As he saw it now, Jackson must have come back seeking revenge!

He peeked cautiously through the windows. It was Jack Jackson all right. He had no trouble recognizing him, even from behind: black sweater, long curly hair, head craned up high as if to better see the hammers striking the strings inside the open piano. When he finally managed to take a better look at the piano player, Rob saw his black pock-marked face and his big bulging eyes and his worst fears were confirmed.

He went down Saint Catherine Street, hailed a taxi and went straight to Fred's house.

"Jack Jackson is back in town!" he yelled out, as soon as he walked in his friend's house.

"Jackson who?" Fred asked.

He raised himself slightly from his bed, which was scattered with crumpled newspapers, and lazily tossed a cigarette butt through an open window.

"Jack. Jack Jackson, the black piano player."

"Can't be! We shipped him out to California."

"I tell you that I have seen him with my own very eyes, and I heard his damned music. He was at The Place, on Stanley Street," Rob said, trying to convince Fred who seemed reluctant to listen to him. "He must have found out that things are a bit different here now. He must have come back to make good on his threat. Do you remember?"

"Listen," Fred said, sliding back into bed. "I don't want to get involved in these things any more. I told you, I have a couple of girls working for me now, I make a good living off of them, and I don't give a damn about drugs or anything else. I don't know how else to tell you: I don't care!"

"But Fred, don't you understand? Jack has come back to get revenge. You and the others lived off of him too, but I was the one who got him hooked. If he finds me, he'll kill me for sure. Don't you understand?"

"What can I do about it, Rob? If he comes after me, I'll be ready and waiting for him. See?" he swiftly pulled a revolver from under his pillow and pointed it at Rob. "It doesn't take much to draw a gun and take him down. Other than defending myself as best as I can, there's nothing else I can do."

"You do not seem to understand, Fred. It's me he is after!"

"Do you need a gun?"

"What for? You know I couldn't shoot at a mouse! We have to find a way to toss him out again. You have to help me, Fred."

"Listen, Rob. I think it is you who could stand a change of air."

"I can't, and you know it. I am not a Canadian citizen yet and I am not free to go where I please. Besides, the police are on to me, they have been for a while now. They're probably tailing me right this minute."

"Okay, okay. Do whatever you want then, go back to Italy if you can, but leave me alone," Fred said impatiently, as he picked up a newspaper and pretending to resume reading.

Rob just stood there, frozen. For a moment he held onto the hope that Fred would come through for him and help him out, just one more time. But Fred kept on looking at the newspaper and smoking his cigarette. He wasn't even acknowledging his presence any more.

"Okay, Fred. You just stay there in your warm bed. But remember, if the others also pull out on me, before Jackson does me in I'll take care of all of you first. Just remember that, friend," Rob yelled, slamming the door behind him.

He didn't feel like doing anything, nor did he feel like seeing anyone. He just wanted to be alone to consider his options.

He found himself walking down Saint Jacques, then on to Girouard, and finally to Park Sherbrooke. He sat down on a bench, and looked around.

A short distance away, there were children playing. They soon got on his nerves, he couldn't concentrate and think. He got up and went to get a cup of coffee at Frank de Rice's.

"It's one o'clock," he told himself, suddenly looking at his watch. "Maybe I'll find him home!"

He took Saint Jacques again, then went down Craig. He continued down Saint Laurent, turned on to Clark Street. He stopped at the back entrance of the Club Saint John and started kicking the door. No one answered. He knocked harder, then stepped back a bit and looked in the direction of a window on the second floor. He could see nothing. He turned and started walking away. He had taken but a few steps when he heard his name being called.

"Rob!"

It was a voice that he didn't recognize. He stopped, startled, but didn't dare turn around, ready for whatever was going to happen.

"Roberto!" he heard again.

Now he recognized the voice that wanted to be friendly. He turned in a flash, happy and relieved.

"Onofrio! Come, quickly. Open the door, I need to talk to you."

Club Saint John is located in the worst section of Boulevard Saint Laurent, near Chinatown between Craig and La Gauchetière. Earlier on, before the Chanteclerc and the Carillon came into existence, the place owed its success to sailors and longshoremen who came up past Notre Dame and Craig, and stopped at the first watering hole on Boulevard Saint Laurent for a beer and a good time. The suburban *canadiennes* used to go there to party the night away, allowing the guys to buy them drinks and popcorn. Some of them turned tricks, having discovered that it was easier to earn a week's pay by spending an extra half hour on their backs in unfamiliar beds.

Onofrio Annibalini opened the heavy door, and let his friend in.

"You want a beer?" he asked Rob.

"Yes, please," Rob said. "I really need one."

"We always need something, even when we believe we have everything," Onofrio said. Then he added kiddingly: "I need to sleep and you come here to wake me up. But that's how life is, I guess!"

"Listen, my good friend. You see . . ." Rob started to say something but then hesitated, as if he were losing his nerve. "If I ask you to put me up in your room for a while, would you do it?"

Onofrio poured some beer in his glass. He was perfectly at home behind the bar counter, opening beer bottles, entertaining friends. Just looking at him, one might think he owned the place, Rob thought. He was pleased to see that Onofrio was doing well, but didn't say anything. He just drank his beer, while waiting for an answer.

"You're in trouble again, Rob, aren't you?" Onofrio asked, avoiding Rob's question.

Rob didn't answer. Even though he had thought of what to say on his way there, he now had second thoughts. He didn't want to lie to Onofrio, but he didn't want to tell him the truth either.

"Not exactly," he finally said, mustering a forced smile. "But there's a woman I'd rather not see for a while. That's all."

"I see," Onofrio said, understanding full well that he was not supposed to ask any more questions.

"And you, Onofrio. How are you doing?" Rob asked, trying to change the subject.

"I am doing quite well, as you can see," Onofrio answered. "I would have thought that you too might have been doing well, that you might have changed your ways. At least, that's what you had told me when you found me this job. What had happened had happened and was water under the bridge. Everything had changed for both of us. 'Onofrio Annibalini, you're a dumb *cafone*,' you said, remember? 'You're a dumb peasant but there is something in you that I could never forget. A dumb peasant, humble and good. And I love you for what you are, notwithstanding all the harm I did you at a time when you needed a friend. Now you have one. And a job too. Everything has changed, for you, and for me.' That's what you said to me, Rob. Don't you remember?"

Rob didn't answer. He poured himself more beer, and continued drinking. Yes, he thought. Everything had changed. But now the dead were coming back to haunt him. It was not his fault: he wanted a change of life, but he wasn't allowed one. Was it his fault?

"Everything did change," he finally said, after a long silence. "The past is dead and gone, and the present is quite different . . . It's just that this woman has fallen in love with me, you see, and I won't stand for it. You see why I have to hide for a while, don't you?"

"I see, and I understand," Onofrio said. "That's why I won't say no. We'll manage."

Years before, when Rob brought him to the Saint John to have him hired as a janitor, Onofrio was a virgin to life in the fast lane. He was a humble and naïve dumb peasant who was appalled when, on entering the club, he saw the murals depicting naked and full breasted Spanish-looking *señoritas*. They were depicted either lying down on an imaginary bed or in a dance pose, a hip thrust out under their long, multicolored Andalusian-style dresses.

On a stage of sorts, a character in his fifties was clowning around, making faces and sucking his cheeks between his teeth. The people seemed to be having a good time, they laughed and clapped hands. Of course, they ate and drank too. A stench of beer, popcorn and other kinds of filth was making Onofrio sick. He was about to suggest to Rob that they leave, when he heard the little man making an announcement.

"Voilà, la starlette de ce soir est une jolie danseuse avec du vrai sang latin dans le corp . . . Voilà, mesdames et messieurs, demoiselle Linda, récemment arrivée de l'Italie!"

"If an Italian dancing girl works here, why shouldn't I?" Onofrio Annibalini told himself. "A job is a job. It's money coming into your empty pockets. Money needed to feed yourself, to pay your debts, to put in the bank and allow to grow, so that old dreams can come true. Dreams make your heart swell with hope and you abandon the comfort of home, the comfort of your own country . . . It's on account of dreams that you have suffered, and when you see your dreams vanish, one by one, it's only natural that you grab onto the last hope, onto the last opportunity."

"Are you working?"

He had been asked the question a thousand times from friends and fellow countrymen alike.

"Are you working?"

His answer had always been a flat *no*: once, twice, a thousand times.

"I have a job, thank God, and money in the bank too. And you, Onofrio, do you have any money in the bank yet?"

Onofrio's gestures always indicated a sad *no*.

"I already have three thousand dollars in savings, thank God. How long have you been here?"

The questions were always the same. Everybody was quick to thank God but no one, in the name of God, lifted a finger to help him out. No one, in the name of God, ever left him alone. They just kept on torturing him with the same stupid and useless questions, over and over again. On these occasions, the more he was asked the more he felt tormented and victimized. He would bite his tongue in order not to start yelling at the people; he would clutch his hands so as not to punch someone in the nose.

So that day he told himself: "Yes. A job is a job!"

He took that job.

It was not heavy work, he even had time to sit down and drink a beer, free of charge. Sometimes he surprised himself looking at the Italian girl as she walked around the lounge swaying her hips like a bitch in heat. She pirouetted around the tables, smiling to the customers who pinched her bottom. Sometimes she stepped on the stage and blew kisses at the people. She was really beautiful, couldn't have been more than eighteen years old. Small but well built, when she danced she moved like she had springs wound up inside. She gyrated her hips round and round, while her bottom rocked back and forth, her stomach undulated in a circular motion, and her half naked breasts bopped up and down.

Everyone shut up when Linda danced. Everyone looked without blinking, including a big fat woman with a mop-like haircut and a manly way about her, who was there every night. She seemed to take the girl in with her eyes, and once in a while she licked her lips with a purplish tongue. Then there was a woman with glasses who sat always alone at a table near the stage. She had a cunning smile printed on her face, and a look of pride in her eyes as she watched Linda dance. Once in a while the girl looked at the woman and winked. Onofrio noticed that the smile of the girl and that of the woman had something in common. Later he came to know that they were mother and daughter.

One night, while looking at Linda's legs, he became oblivious to all else. He was fascinated by the effect that resulted from the gyration of her stomach, the spreading of her legs. His concentration was rudely interrupted when one of the waiters landed on his table. He had been thrown by a large Japanese sailor who had a long scar that went from his forehead all the way down to his left cheek bone. The table and the beer ended up on the floor.

The band stopped playing, the girl stopped dancing and covered her mouth with her hands so as not to yell. The waiter was doubled up in pain, his hands reaching for his body at the height of his kidneys. Two other waiters tried to restrain the bully, but failed. As he freed himself, the bully tried once more to jump on the unfortunate victim.

At that point Onofrio did something he had never done in his whole life. He planted himself in front of the waiter, his legs spread wide just like he had seen done on TV a thousand times. When the Japanese giant tried to throw himself on him, Onofrio delivered such a fierce punch to his stomach, to make him grunt in pain. Then, emboldened by his unexpected success, he delivered a kick to the man's groin. The giant fell to the ground groaning like a pig, while holding with one hand his stomach, his balls with the other.

The two waiters who had intervened before grabbed the sailor by his arms and dragged him outside, where they delivered him to a patrol car, always on duty up and down the street.

"Bravo!" someone said to Onofrio, after order had been reestablished and the little man had gone back onto the stage, performing his usual shenanigans in an effort to make everyone forget what had just happened.

Onofrio took a look at the man who had spoken to him and realized that he was the manager. He smiled, but didn't say a word. The manager asked him to sit down, had two beers brought over, and offered one to him.

"To us!" he toasted.

"To us!" Onofrio repeated, before bringing the bottle to his lips.

The manager seemed to have more experience with beer than Onofrio. He had a rather unique way of drinking from a bottle. He held his tongue against his lower front teeth, and made it act like a stopper; when his mouth was sufficiently full, he pushed his tongue forward against his teeth and stopped the cold and refreshing liquid from coming out of the bottle. At that point, his Adam's apple would bop up and down to let the beer flow.

When he was ready to take another swig, Onofrio decided to experiment. He held his tongue against his lower front teeth and filled his mouth. He then pushed his tongue forward to close the bottle, and sent the beer down. But just as his Adam's apple started to go up and down, he felt a small rivulet of beer trickling down. He removed the bottle from his mouth and dried himself with the sleeve of his jacket.

The manager ordered two more beers.

"A man like you, Mr. Annibalini," he said to Onofrio, "shouldn't be doing the cleaning work here. He should be in charge of keeping the peace and use his fists when necessary."

"I am not very good with fists," Onofrio Annibalini answered, laughing at his earlier prowess.

"It seems to me that you are not just good with fists, you also know how to shut people up," the manager said, looking him in the eyes.

Onofrio smiled again and poured himself some beer: in a glass, this time. He drank, then he looked at his hands.

"No. I know I'm not good with fists," he said, with a tone that was meant not to disappoint the manager. "I just did it for the first time in my life. I don't even know why I did it."

"Would you do it again, if it became necessary?"

"I really don't know," Onofrio answered. Since the manager did not comment, but kept looking at him, as if expecting a more decisive answer, he asked: "Are you offering me a different job?"

"Yes, I am. And with better pay."

"A job is a job," Onofrio answered, smiling. "I mean, it's all the same to me. How much more are you offering?"

"Twenty dollars more," the manager said. Since Onofrio was not answering, he promptly added: "Per week, that is. It's what everyone else pays."

"Yes. But things are different here," Annibalini was quick to point out. "Here, quite often the use of fists is indeed a necessity."

"Shall we say, then, twenty-five?"

"That's better," Onofrio said, unable to hide his happiness.

They bought him a blue suit, a white shirt, a black tie and a pair of black shoes with black socks. When Rob took him to get his bouncer suit, Onofrio looked at his new image in the mirror and hardly recognized himself.

"Who are you?" he asked his reflection in the mirror.

"A new man!" Rob answered. "You are reborn, Onofrio Annibalini, and you are a new man now."

"A man who has led a sheltered life, should always be reborn," Onofrio said. "I have been in an egg shell all my life, but now I came out of it. Yes, I am a new born man."

6

It was seven in the morning and Rob was still sleeping. Onofrio had not gone home yet, accustomed to staying awake during the night and sleeping during the day. That night, in order not to disturb his friend, he decided to take a long walk on Craig Street. When he reached Bleury, he heard newspaper boys crying out to get the attention of the passersby.

"Black man killed on Stanley Street. Behind-the-scenes dealings of night life and prostitution revealed!"

Onofrio bought the newspaper. He was already thinking the worst for Rob. Since he didn't know how to read, he went straight back to the Saint John and up to his room.

"Rob, wake up!" he yelled.

Rob turned the other way and put the blankets over his head. Onofrio pulled them back and shoved the newspaper under his nose.

"Read on. A black man has been killed on Stanley."

Rob sat up, grabbed the newspaper from Onofrio's hands. The headline ran across the columns of the first page. He read that Jack Jackson, the black piano player who had been engaged at The Place for the past several weeks, had been shot three times with a revolver across the entrance of the club. It was also reported that he had recently returned from an extended tour in the United States, and that the assassin had been arrested. His picture was in the paper: it was Fred's!

"I got to go see him," Rob said, while putting his clothes on in a hurry.

"Who?" Onofrio asked.

"Fred."

"Who's Fred?"

"A friend from way back. I have to go see him, I have to find out why he killed the black guy, understand?"

"Sure, I understand. But they're not going to let you see him."

"I know, but I have to try," Rob said, while lighting a cigarette with shaky hands. "I know it will be difficult, Onofrio. I'm going to see my uncle's lawyer, I'm sure he'll find a way to help me out."

When he finally got to see his friend, Rob was all pale and shaking, unable to keep calm. Fred, on the other hand, exhibited a cool, calculated calm. He was disheveled and unshaven, and had two black eyes. When he saw Rob, he rushed to hug him.

"My friend!" he said.

"Is it true?" Rob said. "Is it true and was it you?"

"I had to do it!"

"But didn't you tell me . . ."

"I told you nothing, Roberto," Fred interrupted, his voice eerily calm. "I didn't tell you a thing."

"Be more specific," Rob asked, offering him a cigarette.

Fred took it, then ripped the filter off as he always did since the day he quit smoking the pipe. He lit it and walked to the window.

Rob kept on looking at his friend. He could hardly believe that he was talking to the man who had rid him of Jack Jackson, but shuddered at the thought that Fred might reveal the reason he had committed the murder. If he did, without a doubt he would be incriminated too.

"Jack didn't care much about having been seduced into drugs," Fred said. "He didn't care, drugs helped him become a better player. At least, that's what he used to say. He didn't care because in San Francisco he worked for our own guys dealing drugs. He lived off of drugs and was happy doing it. Drugs were not the reason he had come back to Montreal."

"What was the reason then?" Rob asked.

"It does not concern you, Rob. In any event, you are not the person Jack was after."

"Why did you have to kill him then?"

"Because he didn't come back to get you. As I told you, I wouldn't have killed him for that reason. Fact is, if I didn't get him, he would have had to get me!" Fred concluded. After a moment of silence he added with regret: "Too bad I wasn't able to get away. There was a flight leaving for Columbia, I had everything ready: passport, tickets, luggage, my contacts at the other end, everything . . . Too bad!"

Fred started walking again, calmly and silently as if he were pleased with his actions in spite of the fact that he had failed to get away. After a brief silence, he continued with his story.

"What you don't know is that Jack had a white girlfriend whom he loved very much. Or so he thought. She was probably the only white woman in his life. Hélène, you know her. Hélène Laferrière, *la Parigina*."

"Yes, I know her."

"When Jack became addicted to cocaine, Hélène told me that she had no peace any more. She wanted to leave him, but she was afraid."

"So?"

"So I offered her my protection. One day, while Jack was out, she picked up her things and moved in with me. Jackson found out and put the word out that he would get me killed. This is the true reason why he was shipped to California."

He stopped for a moment, as if to summon strength and courage. Then he continued.

"I introduced Hélène to an old man, an old Italian guy who had certain likings, you know, young girls and all. He paid a lot, he paid well. Hélène gave me a good cut. Things were going very well then. Too bad it's all over now. She is probably very happy alone with her loaded old man."

"What's going to happen now?" Rob asked.

"Don't know. They'll probably hang me!" Fred answered, yet calm, and in a joking way. Then he added, laughing: "If I don't manage to get out of here first, that is!"

"You're not going to squeal on me, are you?"

"Don't worry, there's nothing to squeal about. I am not a coward, you know that."

The conversation ended. They said goodbye and shook hands, looking each other in the eyes.

Back on the street, Roberto lit a cigarette and started to walk. Slowly, as if he were studying his own steps.

Then an idea occurred to him. He hailed a cab and told the cabby to take him to Stanley Street.

7

When he got to Stanley Street, Roberto noticed that everything was back to normal. There was no more confusion than usual, and there were no less people than usual. At Carmen's the regulars were casually sitting and talking, as was normal at that time of the day. At The Place, just under the stairwell outdoors, Tony Ruti was playing chess with the owner, a character in his forties with a long, whitish beard. Dangling from a string around his neck, he had a shark's tooth and two little bells. When he moved, the two little bells chimed like the ones altar boys ring at Mass.

Garcia, a nutty Spanish painter and a regular of the club, watched them play with the usual silly gaze on his face, one foot resting on the chair where the wealthy fat lesbian of Stanley Street was sitting.

Through the window, in the semi-darkness of the lounge one could barely make out the silhouette of two men who were whispering to each other in a corner. Opposite to them, Maddalena Peccatrice was necking with some guy. Rob recognized him as the *peintre chansonnier*, so called because he had actually painted the walls of The Place and of El Cortijo while singing, to entertain the crowd. A lone drinker of 7-UP sat near the band stand, sipping his drink from a straw.

"Move your silly foot," the fat lesbian told Garcia. "You bother me, with that silly grin on your face."

Garcia removed his foot, planted himself in front of the lady and looked at her with squinty eyes.

"Silence," he told her, a moronic look on his face. *"Les lesbiennes ne parlant pas!"*

The woman didn't answer. She just stood there looking at him with an idiotic smile that was meant to imitate his. Garcia stepped away, then tiptoed back as if trying not to attract attention.

"Tiens ça, c'est pour la lesbienne!" he told her with mellifluous voice, while giving her a light slap that was more a caress than a slap.

"Ooooh, ça m'emmerde, le délinquent!" the woman cried out, angry and offended, while at the same time getting up.

Alerted by the woman's scream, the two guys who were inside whispering to each other stepped outside. They took a look at the woman, shrugged their shoulders and went back in, laughing like idiots. They were followed by the 7-UP drinker who, attracted by the commotion, had also come out.

Rob walked up to Tony, put a hand on his shoulder. "Hi, Tony," he said.

"Hi there," Tony answered, without lifting his eyes from the chess board.

"I need a favor."

"Yes?" Tony answered, without breaking his concentration from the queen, his next move.

"Do you have Hélène's address?"

"Hélène who?"

"Listen to me for a moment, then I'll leave you in peace," Rob said, grabbing Tony by the shoulders. "Hélène, *la Parigina.*"

"So?" Tony asked, obviously having not paid much attention to the question.

"Can you give me her address?" Rob burst out, releasing him.

"You could at least say please, couldn't you?" Tony said, now smiling at him.

"Listen, at this moment I can only ask you to please not be an idiot. I have neither the time, nor the desire to fool around. Are you or are you not going to give me her address?"

"Here," Tony said, handing him his address book. "Look for it yourself."

Rob took the book, looked for the address and wrote it down on a piece of paper. He put the book on the table, then left without saying a word.

When he got to Hélène's place, he had to ring several times before she came to the door, wearing a flimsy negligée and nothing else under it. Rob stopped a moment to admire her fine figure: Hélène was not a pretty woman, but she had a wicked body.

"Don't you think it would be better if you came in?" she asked.

"The doorway frames you well," Rob answered, stepping back as if to take a better look at her. "You should have your portrait taken like this, it would be good advertising posted at Carmen's, with your address and phone number. Maybe even your rate."

"Listen, you sonofabitch. If you have come here to insult me, I suggest that you leave before I slam the door on your face."

Rob hesitated a moment, then looked at her from head to toe. He stepped in and closed the door.

"Fred is in trouble," he said.

"Yeah? And how come?" the girl asked, indifferent.

"Because of you, if you ask me."

"Because of me?"

"He killed one of your former lovers."

"Jack," Hélène cried out, her face pale. "It is Jack, isn't it?"

"Yeah. Jack."

"Oh, tabernacle! But why? Why?"

The question was probably addressed more to herself than to Rob. She threw herself on her ruffled warm bed, and started crying.

Rob hadn't given much thought to the girl's feelings and now he was sorry. He didn't expect her to cry for a dead lover, or for a jailed pimp who might end up on the gallows. He walked to the window and lit a cigarette. Unmoved, he listened to the girl's sobs. She was beginning to get on his nerves.

"Who are you crying for?" he gruffly asked.

Hélène didn't answer. She just lay on her bed, face down, her fingers dug into the pillows. Between sobs, she kept on whispering: *"Mais pourquoi? pourquoi?"*

Rob walked up to her. He turned her around and began to dry her tears with a handkerchief. He offered her a cigarette, which she took without saying anything.

"So tell me," he asked, with a tone of concern, while flicking his lighter. "Who did you cry for?"

"I don't know," Hélène answered, her voice unsteady. "I don't know. For Jack or for Fred, maybe for me. I don't know! Can't you understand that?"

Rob put his hand on her naked shoulder and began to caress her, perhaps to be of comfort. Looking at her, he realized that her expression was changing. She looked calmer. She let her cigarette fall to the floor and closed her eyes, letting herself go. She took Rob's free hand, placed it on her chest.

Rob shifted his body around and, after taking her in his arms, tried to make love to her. Hélène pushed him away, and covered herself up as best she could, suddenly modest.

"No, please. Don't do that! I don't want to, I can't," she yelled.

Rob didn't even attempt a second try. He lay down on the bed with his hands locked behind his neck. A moment of silence followed, then Hélène got up, retrieved her scattered clothes from a chair and retired to the bathroom.

She was properly dressed when she came out, a string of pearls around her neck. She looked fresher, prettier even. She sat on the bed again, on the opposite side of Rob.

"You won't even ask me why I couldn't, why I can't?" she said.

"I don't think I really care. The fact that you didn't want to was enough to make me stop. I have always taken my women only when they wanted to, and when they wanted me."

"God only knows," Hélène said. Then she stopped, as if she lacked the courage to continue: "God only knows how much I would like to be able to make love like everyone else."

Rob didn't answer right away, he didn't give much weight to the girl's words. Then he decided to answer.

"I know you are not frigid," he said, "and you are not a lesbo. You have even enjoyed my touching you."

"Yes, I have," Hélène agreed. She stretched out on the bed, then continued: "I have enjoyed it and I loved it. But since I have been with the old man, I have grown so accustomed to the touch of his slimy hands that I cannot make love like I used to. Can you understand? When I am with a man now, the only thing I feel is disgust, I get cramps in my stomach and I want to vomit. Give me another cigarette, please?"

Rob gave her one, and lit another for himself. He did not speak, he just sat there inhaling and trying to make smoke rings as he blew it out. It was as if he were trying to strike a cynical pose. He tried to force a smile even, but it turned into a sneer. Hélène noticed, and turned her head away.

"Why?" she asked.

"I don't know," Rob answered.

"You do not understand, do you?"

"I don't know," Rob answered one more time, without looking at her.

"Rob!" Hélène said, quickly turning towards him. He did not look at her, but she continued just the same. "Rob, I don't want to be mad at you. Not now, anyway. With the old man too, it was like that at first."

Hélène got up and went to the kitchen. She came back with two beers. She gave one to Rob, and started sipping from the other.

"It was like that with the old man too," she continued. "I would feel like vomiting, and he would laugh with great satisfaction. But I got used to it. Then one day, at Carmen's, I met a young man whom I liked very much. When he took me to his place, I suddenly realized that I no longer could have a man and I felt disgust for myself. It was better before, when I was free. I used to spend the whole day on Stanley Street, and didn't have a care in the world. I made love to whomever I wanted and liked, and when I needed money, I allowed myself to be picked up by the johns who cruised Stanley Street in their fancy late model Chrysler, flashing hundred dollar bills. A hundred dollars for an hour of pleasure! I lived well in those uncomplicated days. Then Jack and his cursed music came into my life. When he started using drugs, life became hell with him. So here I am now, with a body that is still young and willing, and my mind telling me that this body is no longer of any use to me."

Rob had been patiently listening to her, a sarcastic smile on his face. He got up, walked to the mirror and straightened his tie.

"*Les femmes de trottoir,*" he said. "It's the most elegant end a woman of the street can come to, so far as I am concerned."

"You don't have the right to insult me!" the girl protested as she stood up and walked up to him. "You don't have the right to insult me just because I am a wretched whore who is disgusted with herself."

"No, I have no right. That's why I am walking away from you. But don't dare come around any more. You know this is sound advice, don't you? If I see you again down Stanley Street, I swear to God something bad will happen to you."

Hélène didn't answer. When Rob moved away, she hurled the beer bottle at her reflection in the mirror. She threw herself on the bed, sobbing, her head buried in the pillows.

Rob stopped a moment to look at her, lit another cigarette and walked to the door. Hélène got up and followed him, as if she wanted to tell him something else. It war Rob who spoke first.

"*Voici,*" he said, touching with gentle fingers the girl's false pearl necklace. "*Voici des gentilles larmes à forme de perles, sur des gentilles perles à forme de larme . . . Voici, la richesse de ton coeur, chérie . . . Mais tu n'es pas qu'une femme de trottoir.* You're nothing but a street walker."

He left, slamming the door behind him.

8

Another winter was coming to an end. Several days had passed since the last snow fall. The thick layer of ice had melted off in the streets, but the cold was still biting. The men were lethargic from idleness, and nature was immersed in a sleep that was always a prelude to reawakening.

In wintertime, when you look at the city from up high and you don't see clouds of smoke from smoke-stacks in the mills nor men at work, and you see the railroad station white and lifeless under a heavy blanket of snow and the lifeless trees bearing the burden of ice and death, then you can really understand the sadness that grips the heart of any new arrived immigrant. Wherever you go, you hear them cursing the heavens and the world. You understand so many things. You feel defeated and useless, a dying animal, a limb broken off of a tree in full bloom. You find yourself cursing the ancient sin and forget that you are a man born to provisional life and to sacrifice. You forget that you are a Christian, a believer in Divine Providence. You become a brute, in body and in spirit, and you know that you could easily kill your neighbor for a mere piece of bread.

Midnight, and not a single car nor a living soul on the Jacques Cartier Bridge. Rob Perussi stood sadly in the darkness of night feeling terribly lonely, abandoned by man and by God. He was fully aware that his life had been simple and easy, he knew that he had never given anything a serious thought and was beginning to regret it. Even now, away from his homeland and in a country he felt he had once loved, he couldn't think clearly about the hardships of life, about the ancient sin.

With his chin resting on the cold steel railing, he watched the river run by. With the melting of the ice-cap that had covered them throughout the long winter, the muddy waters ran swiftly and rather noisily due south; filthy and black in the darkness of the night, they ran impetuously under the bridge and hit its pillars with arrogant force. A foreboding sound rose from below: a sound that after a while impaired Rob's ability to think, stunned him and robbed him of the ability to see clearly in the squalor and darkness of night.

The waters of the Saint Lawrence River were restless that night, as if possessed by a vague but infinite torment. They were murky and restless and yet in them Rob began to see, small, undistinguishable, the outline of a face. He sharpened his sight in an effort to make out the fragmented vision that was floating on the wavy and muddy waters, but wasn't able to do it. His eyes became watery and suddenly a bank of thick fog obstructed his view. He closed his eyes, or perhaps his eyelids grew heavy. Only then was he able to clearly see that the face resembled his own face! It was then too, that the restlessness of the river became his own and was no longer vague: it was a gruesome vision.

And he was afraid!

In a flash of seconds he remembered his friend Line, and a promise he had made to her.

A few days after Fred's arrest, to fight his loneliness and his sense of desperation he had gone to Line's house. He abandoned himself in her arms and made passionate love to her, like he had never made love before in his life. When it was over, he noticed that Line was crying next to him and turned to look at her. Tears were streaming down her cheeks. He put one hand on her nakedness and with the other tried to wipe her tears.

"Leave me alone!" she had said, turning away from him.

She buried her face in the pillow, and he left her alone. He couldn't understand why she was suddenly crying over nothing. Then she started crying louder, almost in desperation. Her hands were tightly clutching the pillow and her chest rose and fell to the rhythm of her sobs. He passed his hand through her hair and began caressing and gently kissing her naked shoulders. He wanted to console her.

"No, please," she had begged between sobs.

At that point Rob got up from the bed and began dressing. While looking for his socks, he turned and noticed that Line was wiping her tears with the back of her hand. The moment she saw him looking at her, she turned the other way to avoid his eyes.

"Why are you acting like this?" he asked her.

Line refused to answer, lowered her head and held it between her hands.

"Answer me!" he had asked sternly.

"I don't know. I really don't know why I cried. But I feel like crying and crying and crying, and to talk like I never talked in all my life and . . . and to make love again and again as if this was the last time."

"I don't understand."

"I know. Men usually don't understand these things, do they?" Line said without looking at him.

"Why aren't you looking at me?" he asked.

"Because you wouldn't understand what I would like to tell you. You men are all the same. You take a girl in your arms, you make love to her, then you couldn't care less about her, you treat her like a whore."

"Why are you saying this?" he asked in a stern tone, almost an order. "I have never treated you that way. You have no right to say that, and you know it."

"Yes, I know," Line yelled, finally turning to look at him. "I know I have no right to talk this way because I am a whore, because I like to make love, because I brought you to my house. Isn't that so?"

"You are not the only one who . . ."

"I'm not, am I?" Line interrupted. "I'm not the only one because we women are all the same too, aren't we? But what we are looking for isn't any different than what you are looking for, you know? It's just that we . . ."

Line couldn't go on. She started sobbing again, hiding her face in the pillows.

He had stood quiet and still, waiting for more: an explanation, perhaps. But nothing came. He was suddenly curious. Driven by the desire to satisfy his curiosity he pretended to be moved, much more than he actually was at the moment. He ran his hand through her hair again and lifted her chin.

"Go on," he encouraged her. "It's just that you . . ."

"I won't!" Line said, pushing him away. "Why do you want to make me talk? You wouldn't understand anyway, would you?"

"You're so sure!" he had replied. Then he made her lie on her back on the bed again. "You say I couldn't understand but I want to. Couldn't you help me understand?"

Line turned over, her face covered with her hands so as not to look him.

"I can't, I'm ashamed," she finally said. "I'm ashamed because what I want to say to you has nothing to do with what we have just done. It's different. Can't you understand?" she yelled, as she sat up again.

He took his tee shirt off and lay next to her, his hands locked behind his head. Line remained sitting up on the bed for a bit longer, then turned towards him and lay next to him with her head on his chest. She began to kiss him.

"You see, I'm just a whore. You are right to despise me," she whispered, as if to herself, while kissing him. "I'm a whore and I like to make love. Go on, call me a whore, why don't you call me a whore?"

"Stop it!" he yelled.

He got up, forced her on her back once again, then he slapped her on the face with the back of his hand.

"Yes!" Line mumbled, and started to cry again.

He remembered that he hadn't been moved by her tears. He had laid down on the bed again, but far from her. Eventually, he fell asleep.

When he woke up, a few hours later, Line was sleeping next to him and he looked at her. She looked tired, her face moist from crying. She seemed to be relaxed and satisfied, in body and spirit. To him, she had looked more beautiful than ever.

He felt an impelling need to put his hand on the spot that was the source of his desire and to caress the hollow of her legs, a place he remembered to be smooth as velvet. He also felt the impelling need to touch her breasts with his lips, to feel her move under him, to hear her moan and then to feel her come again while he embraced her with all his might. But sleeping as she was, she looked so vulnerable and innocent that he didn't have the heart to touch her. On her lips, even as she slept, she wore the mischievous smile that he loved so much.

Line stirred in her sleep. He looked at her again, then leaned over and kissed her on the mouth. Her lips opened, as if she were dreaming. Then she opened her big, expressive green eyes, stretched and put her arms around his neck, wishing to be kissed again.

It didn't turn out to be a soft, sensuous kiss. Their lips touched only so lightly, as if his lips were gently resting on hers, delicately sipping a rose nectar.

"You have been awake?" Line asked.

"Yes, about ten minutes."

"How long did we sleep?"

"I don't know," he answered, tenderly caressing her small firm breasts. "I don't know," he said again, kissing the tip of her nose. "But it doesn't matter now, does it?"

Line was again becoming aroused next to him. She was warm with passion, and that same passion driven smile was stamped all over her face, two sexy dimples on her cheeks. He kissed those dimples, he himself crazy with passion. His hand, rendered once again skillful and impatient by his excitement, was sliding down from the back of the her neck past her breasts, past her belly, intent on reaching the source of his passion. He could feel her flesh under him becoming ever more demanding and receptive.

Line's moans made him understand that she was ready for him. Her body opened up and engulfed him while she groaned with pleasure. His body became hers and she drew it to her with warmth and kindness.

"I really think you should be able to talk to me now," he told her, afterwards. "You feel okay now, don't you? You do trust me a bit more, don't you?"

"I don't know," Line answered, lowering her head. "But I feel that I have to. I feel that you have to understand me now."

As they looked in each other's eyes, he remembered his past, his womanizing days devoid of love for anything and anyone. He was suddenly taken by a desire to love and to be loved, to feel close to someone and to feel a woman near him, a woman that was his, made just for him.

He remembered far away places that he had never loved. He tried to see with his mind's eye the face of just one of the women that had passed through his life without love, but was unable to do it. He felt defeated by something vague and unknown, yet at the same time real and powerful that made his temples throb.

Line had noticed and said: "What are you thinking?"

It was as if she had awakened him from a sleep that had lasted a lifetime: someone else's lifetime.

"What?" he asked. "Oh, I'm sorry. I wasn't thinking about anything in particular. Just thinking: about myself, about you, about this world of ours. Nothing in particular."

"I understand."

"I was thinking, perhaps, about the emptiness enclosed within all things that makes life itself so full of . . . you know, of nothing but emptiness. I have no idea what it all means, but that's what I was thinking."

He stopped talking and she looked at him with admiration, her big eyes wide open. He bent to kiss her, then he took her hand and squeezed it hard, interlocking his fingers with hers.

"And you," he then asked, finally smiling to her. "What did you want to tell me?"

"I don't know. I don't even feel like talking any more. Maybe . . . maybe I just wanted to tell you that everything with you has been so different."

"Different, in what way?"

"While we were making love the first time, for instance, I felt like I was in the process of being reborn. I felt like I was reborn attached to you and the more I had the feeling that I was attached to you, the more I felt good and alive. As your passion grew while we were making love, so did I. I felt as if I were growing up and then in the end . . ."

"In the end?"

"I don't know if you can understand, if it has ever happened to you. In the end I felt that I was finally born, reborn, that is, and I was different, better than what I had been until that moment. Do you understand? But why am I telling you these things?"

"Yes, why?" he asked. He touched her lips with his, then once again asked: "Why, indeed?"

"Do you think you can understand?"

"I think I can. For an instant you probably felt what I felt, what everybody should feel at least once in a lifetime. We will get away from Montreal, Line. I'll take you with me to Italy, to Rome. We will forget everything and everyone, start a new life there."

He had understood that in order to find himself he had to overcome something stronger than him. He had to meet that something that he called boredom head on. His boredom, he knew, had its roots in Italy. "But first," he told himself, "I must look for an honest job and hold on to it for a while."

In his quest for an honest job, he had become like everyone else and finally felt like everyone else: a frustrated immigrant, out there looking for a job. Frustrated and impatient, neurotic, cursed by bad luck and condemned to failure, while at the same time enjoying a happiness, with Line, that could never be complete without the security of a job and a peaceful life. He began to understand the unhappiness of his fellow immigrants, their empty words, their sense of futility, their desperation.

He did not like any of it.

From the darkness of the Jacques Cartier Bridge he looked again at the image reflected in the churning muddy waters of the Saint Lawrence River below. It was a sickly and suffering face, desperation stamped all over it. It was a face that even he could not recognize, because it had been changed by an unexplainable tenderness: his face!

He realized in that flash of seconds that he was alone in his fight against a bitter destiny and began repeating to himself words that were a cry for help, words that others had uttered to him in the past while he was listening with unsympathetic ears and hidden sarcasm.

Those words were in his mind, on his lips, as were the tears now streaming down from his very own eyes. The thought of suicide he had seen, unmoved, in the pale faces of others was now his too while in his mind he once more saw people's trembling lips utter words of vengeance and death.

Under the spell of these thoughts he shuddered, overtaken by sudden fear. He was lost, alone in a world he had never been able to fully understand.

"Heeeeelp!" he heard someone yell.

His heart stopped. His fingers wrapped tightly around the bars of the railing. As his nails dug into the cold flesh of his hands, he felt the physical pain spread throughout his body.

"Heeeeelp!"

He heard that scream again and felt a burning sensation in the palm of his hands. His fingers let go of the railing and slowly, with great effort, opened up. He moved his hands up to his face and looked at them, wide eyed and desperate. Overtaken by fear, he covered his face with shaking hands.

The voice calling for help was now loud and clear, and again his hands grabbed the bars of the railing. Shaking all over, he looked below at the river waters.

"Heeeelp!"

There, in a patch of clear water, he could see some-thing or someone move: a human body fighting for life! The water was carrying that body towards the bridge, then the body disappeared under it. Rob took his trench coat off and ran to the opposite side of the bridge, while desperately calling for help. He climbed over the railing with the agility of a wild animal, one leap and he was down.

On hitting the water, he suddenly felt physically and mentally stronger than ever before. With all his newly found strength he started swimming toward the form he had seen from the bridge, and in which he had clearly seen a human face. He reached that form, put his arms around it.

It was a log!

He let it go and started swimming to the safety of the shore. He climbed the river bank and started running.

He was frightened.

9

One evening, uninvited, *compare* Petrilli walked in on Onofrio Annibalini at the club, with Carmela and their two young sons.

Since he had started working at the Club Saint John, Onofrio had been able to pay off his debt with the *compare* and had moved from his home so as not to be a bother any longer.

"I shall not be disturbing you any more, *compare*," he had told him one evening. "Please, accept my apologies for the inconveniences and the embarrassment I may have caused you and your family."

"But what are you saying, *compare* Onofrio!" Petrilli said, suddenly concerned.

They insisted that he continue to stay with them. It was no bother, really, they told him. On the contrary, he had become part of the family.

"Yeah, sure!" Onofrio thought. "Now that I can pay, it is convenient to have my fifteen extra dollars per week and they reward me with a smile. But when I had no money, when I was out of work, I was a burden and received a frown every time we sat at the table to eat, and every time I brought the fork with a morsel of food to my mouth. But now that I have a job and I have money, now I'll go!"

So he did, he left. At the Club Saint John he was offered a room on the second floor, free of charge. That room had become his home: a home better than "home."

The Petrillis had just taken a seat when Line came in. Onofrio saw that she was alone so he excused himself from the Petrillis and went to meet her. She looked pale and withered, rather sickly he thought.

"Rob, where is he?" Onofrio asked.

Line didn't answer. Onofrio held her hands but she just looked at him, empty-eyed and unable to talk. It was as if her mouth was refusing to make a sound. Her lower lip quivered, but wouldn't open up.

"Why aren't you talking?" Onofrio asked, while trying to calm her. "Has anything happened?"

"Yes!" Line finally said. "It's horrible!"

"What do you mean, what is it?" Onofrio asked, anxious.

Line opened her purse, pulled something out of it and with trembling hands handed it to Onofrio. She wiped her tears, trying not to cry. But she was sobbing.

"Two airline tickets," Onofrio said. "Where were you going?"

"Lima, Peru. Rob couldn't stand it here any more. In the last few days he had been acting crazy. They refused to release his passport, but he tried to get away just the same. At the airport, while I was in line to get my documents checked, he tried to avoid passport control and then . . ."

She stopped talking, started crying all over again. Onofrio looked at her without saying a word. He held her hands tightly, trying to give her strength to go on.

"Then I heard two gunshots," Line said. "I made my way through the crowd and I saw Rob on the ground, under the airplane ramp. The police had recognized him. He asked me to tell you that he wasn't able to do what you had told him to do. He couldn't shrug away his lot of misfortune, or *disgrazia*, as you called it. He said he had become Roberto once more, and had to pay dearly for his *disgrazia!*"

"Once, a long time ago, Rob told me that he wanted to go back to Italy," Onofrio said somberly. "He will go back. Late perhaps, but he will. I am going to take care of it myself. Where did they take him?"

"At the General Hospital. He died there."

"I'll take care of everything, Line. You go home now. I'll come later on to see how you're doing," Onofrio told her.

He called one of the waiters and asked him to take the girl home. Then he went back to the *compare* and his family.

"My dear *compare*, I hardly recognize you!" Petrilli told him, after a calculated pause that was meant to be a reproach. "You have betrayed our ancestors and the decency of our people. You better watch out, *compare*, the curse of the dead is a terrible one to drag around."

His wife didn't say much, other than the good evening when she first saw him. Their sons had gone to sit at another table away from them and were enjoying the show. The master of ceremonies was in the middle of announcing Linda's act and the *comare* opened her eyes in horror.

"What is this?" she said, crossing herself twice. "An Italian dancing girl, naked and all?"

"What's wrong with that, *comare*?" Onofrio replied, unable to hide his reaction to the news he had just been given.

It was indeed true, he thought. You can come to life bearing the curse of misfortune on your shoulders. He used to say it in jest, but now he knew that it was really true.

"Dear *compare*, you dare ask me what is wrong with it?" the *comare* asked.

"Sure!" Onofrio said quite simply. "The girl's own mother is here. There, see her, the woman down there?"

he added, pointing towards Linda's mother. "It was she who brought her daughter here. She wanted to make sure that the girl got the job. Since the girl was reluctant to raise her skirts up to show her shapely legs, the mother did it for her, right here, in front of everyone."

Onofrio knew that it wasn't true, but he didn't care; they wouldn't have been able to understand anyway. The Petrillis were still living sheltered lives, and still bore the curse of *la disgrazia* on their shoulders. Onofrio was amused by the look of shock on their faces. He enjoyed seeing them flaunt their false modesty. They who had been themselves so disloyal with him!

"In Italy you would never see such a thing," *compare* Petrilli said. "A good woman stays home. If she lives in the village, she sits and knits; if she lives on the farm, she gets up with her husband when the cock crows and goes to till the soil like a man. Though women might bear their young like rabbits, they still raise them right."

"When one of the females turns out to be as beautiful as this one here," the *comare* Michelina added, motioning to the dancer, "they jealously guard her, like the thousand *lira* bill husbands hide under a brick, for safe keeping."

"Is that so?" Onofrio said, a clever smile on his lips, the kind of smile that could only come from his new self. "Just what is Italy, *comare*, and where is it? We left it, remember? It is far, far away now, on the other side of the ocean. Do not forget, *comare*, that it is when we abandon our country that we betray our origins and loose our identity. We don't regain it until we shed our old clothes and don new ones. Just like I did, see?" he added, getting up to show off. "I did it! Not only do I have something new on the outside, I also have new stuff on the inside. Now I am Onofrio Annibalini but before . . . who was I before?"

"I hardly recognize you, *compare* Onofrio!" the *comare* said, pursing her lips and acting offended.

"Really, *comare?* You say that you can hardly recognize me?" Onofrio said. "But you, my dear *comare*, you never knew me. The man you knew was not this Onofrio Annibalini. He was just a poor devil and a *cornuto*, a cuckold like thousands, millions of others around the world. You talk about Italy, about the thousand *lire* bill hidden under the brick? You make me laugh, *comare!* Just what might you get with your thousand *lire* that you hide under the brick, what exactly?"

"Now you dare ask us what's a thousand *lire*," the *compare* commented, scandalized.

"Yes, tell me: what's a thousand *lire?* What can you buy with your thousand *lire* hidden under a brick?"

"It's nothing, Onofrio, and you can't buy much with it," Petrilli answered rancorously. Then, after he thought about meager rewards of the past, he added: "It's nothing, because it is something whose value you no longer recognize. You can't remember now, *compare*, what the worth of a thousand *lire* is. But when you're sitting by the fireplace chewing on a piece of toasted cornbread and anchovies, with the little wine you have left at the bottom of the flask, then you think about that thousand *lire* bill which is nothing, as you say, but still you keep it under a brick. In the evening you enjoy taking it out and looking at it, alone in the stable, by the light of an old oil lamp. You don't remember how good you feel, how much of a different man you are . . . You feel so good because you know that when you die, your loved ones have enough money to pay for your funeral and have the cobbler dye the tops and the soles of your old shoes."

"If your son dares to talk back to you," the *comare* added, "you are free to raise your voice, even take your belt off to show him who is boss. Can you not remember this, *compare?*"

Onofrio looked at them and started laughing. Then he looked in the direction of Linda's mother. She was sitting at her usual table, with her potato chips and a coke.

"No, I said it before: it is when a man leaves his country that he betrays his origins and begins to understand life. That woman down there, the mother of the dancing girl, she has understood," he said, pointing to Linda's mother. "She was made to understand and she too no longer lives a sheltered life. People like us, born into a sheltered life, are burdened by a curse that we call misfortune, *la disgrazia*. A person who doesn't leave the safety of his shelter and doesn't shrug off his *disgrazia* will be forever known as unlucky or worse, *disgraziato*. To shrug it off you have to be willing to do anything, *compare*. Anything at all, you understand? You have to be willing even to die!"

He had Rob in his mind, of course. And the more he thought of his friend, the meaner he sounded. At least to the *compare* and to the *comare* who suddenly got up and left, tail tucked between their legs, unable to hide their disappointment.

"Yes!" Onofrio Annibalini repeated to himself, once he was alone again. "We are born with the burden of *la disgrazia* on our shoulders, and if we don't shrug it off, in time we will be called unlucky, *disgraziati*. Everybody could call me *disgraziato* in the past. But now, now no one can! No one dares!"

Linda's mother had been joined by someone at her table. The man who had joined her appeared to be a bit drunk. While laughing, he let one of his hands casually fall on the woman's thighs and pinched them.

The lady smiled, but didn't move.

AFTERWORD

JOURNEY AND MATURITY OF PIETRO CORSI

An Italian writer or an Italo-American writer?

1. The dilemma. Sorrow, rancour, shame. Then quietude. Life continues, it has taken a turn on the road. The turn is called *emigration*.

At the start it's called with another name: torture: A torture to think in one language and to try to write in another. The years pile up on each other, the mind reacts to commands but no longer out of instinct or out of habit to that instinct: you think in Italian and you write in Italian. You think in English and you write in English. There are always mistakes in writing whether in the former or the other language. And that depends, above all, on the fact that the writer cannot, must not err.

Now another drama sets in: living with a dictionary close at hand.

Pietro Corsi, and his colleague who is now discussing him, were born in the same Italian town, Casacalenda, in the Molise region. Both were educated in Italy and lived there almost up to middle-age, that age which Dante calls *"nel mezzo del cammin di nostra vita,"* the midway of this our mortal life.

With alternate luck we have left behind there books published with our name and surname. Then the sudden lightning flash, the uprooting, the emigration: starting all over again from scratch.

Will we or won't we make it?

Pietro and I have often asked ourselves this question. For what a writer wants more than anything else is the most difficult thing of all, namely the memory of who he was, or who he is or he will be in a situation that is no longer called *exile*, as in Dante's or Foscolo's time, but *relocation*, which is another way of saying "change face and fortune."

Emigration is a pitiless therapy, many have been through it: it suffices to recall Conrad and Nabokov. But it does not cease to frighten. Am I now an Italian or an Italo-American writer living in America and writing in Italian, sojourning in Italy and writing in English?

The answer could lie perhaps in the assertion that the writer identifies himself with the language in which he writes, not with the country in which he lives or on which he often writes. B. Traven wrote in German, but he lived in Mexico and depicted Mexican life. But the Mexicans now would like to claim him as their writer and, indeed, he is studied in the schools: in translation!

The dilemma persists: who am I? where am I? how and why do I write?

2. The lesson. The hyperbole is the lesson, and this comes to us from Dante.

"In quella parte del libro de la mia memoria" – in that part of the book of my memory: thus begins the *Vita Nova*.

And further:

La dispietata mente, che pur mira
di retro al tempo che se n'è andato,
da l'un de' lati mi combatte il core;
e 'l disio amoroso, che mi tira

ver lo dolce paese c'ho lasciato,
d'altra part'e con la forza d'Amore;
ne lungiamente i' possa far difesa.

("The pitiless mind that still looks / backward to the time that has gone, / from one of the sides assails my heart; / and the loving desire that draws me / to the sweet country that I left / from the other side it is with the force of love,/ nor do I feel within me sufficient courage / to defend myself for long against them.")

From Dante we have learned that writing, whoever you may be, and in whatever language you may write, is above all *remembering*. But far from one's roots writing and remembering (*remembering* stands also for *confessing*, confessing like *loving*) are matters so arduous that they can be undertaken and, at times, even brought to fruition only after having passed through an infinite and lacerating attitude of inner research.

Analogies?

The "dark forest," the unknown havoc; the "hill," the Northwest Passage; "my guide," Virgil, will perhaps be another emigrant or son of emigrants accompanying you in his club or around his neighborhood to you pointing out what constitutes the "new life." Always a ghetto, at the start, your own, personal hell.

Fredi Chiappelli, who dedicated his own life to studies of Dante and Machiavelli, situates Dante's *Incipit vita nova* at the age of eighteen. Turning the historical data up on its head we, instead, say that it began at the age of thirty-five with the other *Incipit* to Cangrande when the memory becomes a filter after the years of hunting parties and errors, when one has come to terms with oneself and there is no longer a possibility of fictions or games in the manner of the *dolce stile*, the sweet style.

Is this how masterpieces are born?

Pietro Corsi learned from Dante that the *incipit* begins precisely when one fears that one has forever lost both *"lo dolce paese c'ho lasciato"* and the ability to communicate, to live like a normal, universal person, stammering now in Dante's vernacular (at night and in total solitude) in a land frequented by the vernacular of Chaucer. But by thus stammering and eating hamburgers (*l'altrui pane,* the bread of others) one has sought for the hopeless growth, that light that shines at the end of the tunnel.

Memory has ramifications in the darkness.

3. The passage. The personal history of the writer Pietro Corsi (he has been living in Los Angeles, California for more than thirty years), whether he be an Italian or Italo-American writer, is an exemplary one.

He has written a novel in English, *Sweet Banana*, and still in English a couple of international cookbooks that could arouse Marcella Harzan's envy. But the books that count, written in Italian, are novels dealing with the theme of emigration, of the Italian who has emigrated to lands far away from the ancient *borgo selvaggio,* primitive village of Leopardian memory. And these lands – Canada, Mexico, the United States – although different from each other in language and culture, have the same meaning. They present themselves with the same face, first the face of darkness, then that of light. And they translate themselves in revolution and fable and are, above all, a bridge, a sanguineous link almost sacred between Europe and America, humanism and adventure, metascience and meditation.

We have known each other for so many years I cannot invent lies of any kind of mastery over Pietro Corsi: he lives his life and I mine, he writes in his way, and I in a way peculiar to me. Apart from the human affection, the real fondness that unites us is the spider-web of writing, his and mine, Italians of Italy and, at the same time, Italians of America. Others exchange letters out of habit and we, out of the very same habit, exchange manuscripts. Publishing has become secondary. What really counts is that we have known how to write: that is, *to see, to perceive, to register, to translate, to create, to recreate* with respect for the real but with fantasy and humor, passion and philosophy.

This attitude of ours could be misunderstood as *art for art's sake.* Nothing could be more mistaken: one still looks around for a publisher, one still seeks the public, the reader. But, I repeat, the writer who has emigrated is guilty of being an immigrant: he is under constant prosecution and scrutiny. Although belonging, he does not belong, neither to this land nor any more to the land whence he comes. What to do? Exchange manuscripts, what else?

4. The night writer. Pietro Corsi reminds me – with the due differences, with the distorted myopia – of a poet very dear to me, Wallace Stevens, whose life unfolded in a skyscraper in Hartford, Connecticut, as the Vice-President of an insurance company. Known in the literary world, he was unknown as a major poet to his clients. When he died, and I was among those accompanying his hearse, some of the rich ladies were amazed to discover on that particular occasion that Wally was, in fact, this and that, but primarily a poet.

And Pietro also reminds me, with the same due differences and distorted myopia, of William Carlos Williams, another poet, but a doctor by profession.

Pietro Corsi has been the Executive Vice-President of a famous steamship company specializing in cruises, and the passengers of his ships know only his cookbooks. But they don't call him "writer" since cookbooks are considered manuals. Even Artusi who, explaining his recipes, has applied the writer's art to them. And precisely in the manner of Stevens and Williams, Corsi is a nocturnal, a night writer, one who tries to justify his life "solely" through his creative works: the novel, the short story, poetry. Whether later someone may read or not read them is a different matter.

Pietro has written and written, and he has published and published. He is better known in Italy than America, obviously. But his books wander about like orphan children of the father. A father, according to the rules, should be present at religious functions, at weddings, at baptisms, at funerals, at birthday parties. For a writer it is important to be in his "own" ambience, in arm's reach of a publisher or the literary agent. But it's not so for the emigrant. The anger that marks emigration is to be alone.

One day, many years ago, visiting him in his office at Century City in Los Angeles, I asked him: "What were you looking for, what were you searching for when you left Molise? Money, success, steaming secretaries like these Carol's, Marissa's, Colleen's of yours?"

"To save myself!" he replied.

"From Molise?"

"I wanted to commit myself to time with its intrinsic salvific value."

"But time is fluid."

"To be sure," he replied. "Yet one can always gather, in the instant in which we live, a certain measure of eternity. And this comes, perhaps, from writing, by continuing to travel, that is to say, by writing . . ."

This is the measure of the nocturnal writer. And Pietro Corsi wrote and wrote in the years while directing the shipping company without making it weigh upon anybody. He published his first two books clandestinely.

He did not have a list of critics in his pocket, nor any particular acquaintances in the literary world.

However, he was content that the object of his efforts existed. It sufficed to his hypertrophy of the I. And also because the latter is accentuated in emigration.

The immigrant writer lives with a half severed head. But he doesn't give up. He continues to think, to act, to construct. A day goes by, a year goes by, autumn comes, comes summer: perhaps, who knows, we have finally arrived at the end of the tunnel.

But have we arrived?

5. *In exitu.* In his essay on Pietro Corsi, Fred L. Gardaphé of Chicago, who is highly knowledgeable on Italo-American writers and *letterati*, has brought to light certain aspects of Corsi's first novel, *La Giobba,* that link him to the Italian-American tradition of social investigation, expounded with a political-polemical slant with respect to the American situation of the 1930s by Di Donato's classic *Christ in Concrete.* Gardaphé also links the inherent social history of *La Giobba* on work or not working in order to survive or not live, with another Italian-American classic, *Wait Until Spring, Bandini,* by John Fante.

Exactly. History repeats itself. But the following differences discernably course through those novels and Corsi's novel: Onofrio Annibalini was born in Italy and emigrated to Canada after the Second World War, knowing neither English nor French, only his Molise dialect. Unlike Di Donato's and Fante's characters who were born (and actually bestir themselves) in an America (that is their homeland) before the Second World War, using phrases and proverbs culled from the dialect of their emigrant fathers that no longer links them, unfortunately, either to Italy or to Italian culture.

Gardaphé notes this friction on the binary of a negative megaparanoia that seems to bind together emigrants, those of yesterday and those of today, beyond historical structures of time and space. And this megaparanoia is called *alienation*. To use a language, to find another. The real drama is the alienation. One loses the memory of who one is. And this sums up all that which a modern writer like Corsi wants to avoid.

La Giobba consists of two stories that become one novel by way of mysterious plots. Particularly the first one, that revolves around Onofrio Annibalini, is admirably drawn tight in its form of *status nascendi*, of becoming. And this for the writer as such and his characters as testimony of his time.

In this book emigration, including its sorrow, becomes a celebration of that which Dante reminds us of when he cites the psalm *In exitu Israel de Aegypto*. The central character becomes a symbol of an existential situation, emigration, that transcends classes and origins. It is here precisely that the problem of the emigrant writer again comes into play: only by universalizing is it perhaps still possible to live emigration, to stay within its fold and at the same time remain outside it.

He who understands understands, says the Naples of G.B. Vico: *Non omnibus datum sed qui potest capire capiat*. For "to understand" is like "understanding oneself."

6. Brutal mellow Mexico. The personal history of Annibalini was first published in installments in the newspaper of the Italian colony of Montreal, *Il Cittadino canadese*. Later, at my suggestion, it was published in one volume for which I wrote the introduction. Literature is a private event before it becomes a public occasion, and testimony can at times be of positive help to criticism as it gleans in that human spiritual and passional underground which

has tormented the man the writer before depositing itself in the literary work.

Corsi's Canada quickly lost itself in optical dissatisfaction since emigration had no glimmer of personal light for the writer now hungry for experiences. Pietro came to see me in New York where I lived in 1961 and from there, just like Ishmael, he embarked on a ramshackle ship which brought him on a tour of the Antilles, Venezuela and the Caribbean, finally dumping him on the burning beaches of Mexico where he remained immolated between *aguardiente* and *tequila*, peones and *licencias* as well as *licenciados*. Here begins Corsi's Mexican investigation which, later, dictated to him books of a dense obscure passion for that land devastated by political corruption and endemic poverty, but as lively as fireworks in love and perdition.

These books poured out like volcanoes in a constant flow: *Sweet Banana* (1984), *Ritorno a Palenche* (1986), *Lo sposo messicano* (1989) and *Amori tropicali di un naufrago* (1990).

Emigration in these books assumes hallucinatory aspects: in *Sweet Banana* it is expressed in a brothel in Acapulco; in *Ritorno a Palenche* in the archeological dress of the use and abuse of Mayan culture; in *L'uomo-dio* (forgotten in galleys in the publisher's house in Campobasso up to this moment) in superstitions, ignorance and blackmail; in *Lo sposo messicano* in the desire for an impossible love in the arms of the "usual" Mexican revolution; in *Amori tropicali di un naufrago* in the construction of an essential life in perfect union with the landscape at first the foe, then vanquished and become dear through the genius of labor and the mysterious hand of politics.

Sweet Banana, Corsi's first novel in English (which one year later was rewritten and published in Italian under the title *Un certo giro di luna*), is based on authorial tones of a maniacal intimacy, presenting pseudoporno scenes and intense, morbid descriptions bathed, I would say, by both the Mexican landscape and the protagonist Paco. Deep sorrow surfaces there in the superficiality of the "game" which is that of love bought and sold in the intense and crazy tourist summer of a crazy Acapulco with its knives and languors.

This novel is a saga of sensibility and sensuality just grazing the skin. But the motor behind the whole is the immigrant called Paco, in truth a woman imprisoned in the body of a man, who suffers the pains, the humiliations and the indignities that happen, or could happen, only to a gay person who lives in a wholly discriminatory, macho society. But Corsi brings to his characters – who indeed are symbolic masks such as Conchita, China, Yolanda, Maria, Gringa, and to men like Mister Fred and the Custom Inspector – a depth of observation and a social and religious spectroscopic scrutiny.

The subject matter in itself in some way recalls a novel of the Italian 1960s, *Natale in casa di appuntamento*, by Ugo Moretti (1963). Corsi, however, internationalizes that subject matter, making almost a mystique of it, and infuses therein a certain political judgment in respect to sexual liberty. At the time he wrote the book, there was not yet talk of AIDS. Paco dies of it, but the reader is induced to believe that the cause of his death was "mysterious" infarct.

7. *Por qué vives?* Corsi's investigation continues and brings us to Palenque, Chiapas region, in the forests of southeastern Mexico among temples and lianas and rubber cutters, a journey that Pietro and I made together in 1962 and which remains indelibly impressed on our minds. But, luckily for him, Corsi succeeded in transforming the whole into literature where on every breath-

ing soul dominates the landscape, the burnished green of the leaves of the labyrinthine forests in which it rains and rains, but the bare head that wanders among the Mayan sarcophagi is never cooled off by it: the rain, remains suspended in the heights of the millenary trees that conceal the sky and defy the temples.

Pietro does not relate our story as travelers, but rather insinuates himself with a perturbing precision into the ambiguous Indo-American plasma, alternating between irony and repulsion, along with a heart-rending mediation on the cultural roots of its people, their hunger, their faith. The latter, precisely, faith – on which the writer insists, as if he himself personally is seeking it – is lost and regained with a voracious tenacity.

Perhaps Graham Greene, of whom Corsi is an admirer, could have written a book like this with a deep religious thematic. But Corsi gives it his own stamp as seeker, as emigrant, who in every particle of the world sees a suffering flake of his and our expatriate state.

It is the contemporary (perennial) story of poor miserable children sold for adoption, of the sorrow of a human sterility rich in money but not in biological substance. And of a little church in the jungle earmarked for destruction which, despite the perverse poverty of the natives, still functions as a haven of spiritual restoration, like a beacon on the reef to the bark lost in the billows. It is the story of the Browns, a monied but sterile married couple, who in every way feel in themselves, and in an overpowering way, the need to have roots in the world, generations that will follow and remember them, even if these roots are acquired at the price of barter deal.

There is no political proposal: the polemical debate (at that time) between Capitalism and Marxism, rich and poor, big and small, cultivated and uncultivated, or Tony the Tiger or the supreme hormone Popeye against the flaccid American businessman. *Ritorno a Palenche* is a book of a subtle religious seduction in the rediscovery of the pagan myth in which the Mayan anthropology surfaces like a desert rose and envelops but without pressing, a jungle of passion and of mute shrines, the sarcophagi and the temples of the forest, the tropical rain and the secret cry of the heart.

Por qué vives tú? Why do you live? Have you a reason for living?

This is the essence of the book: it treats of a novelized reasoning that leans on hope.

8. Hope. This narrative-philosophic perseverance that in Christian terms we call *Spes*, hope, rolls up all the work of Pietro Corsi, including his last two novels, *Lo sposo messicano* and *Amori tropicali di un naufrago*.

One of the teachers I admired most at the Sorbonne when I passed through Paris on the morrow of the Second World War, the venerable Gaston Bachelard, perhaps would be able to summarize the ethics of these last two novels by Corsi in a religious parable but, alas, for many readers it would be abstruse, obstinately intellectual.

I shall quote it anyway.

> In their great actions the living Male and Female are King and Queen. Under the sign of the double crown of the king and of the queen, as the king and queen cross their lily they unite the feminine and masculine forces of the cosmos. King and Queen are sovereigns without a dynasty. They are two conjoined powers, devoid of reality if we isolate them (*La poetique de la rêverie*, Paris: PUF, 1960).

A collection could be deduced from these two above-mentioned books (important as they are, I shall not discuss them here for lack of space – they need a "space" proper to them) on the basis of certain short stories (still not known to the public but already mentioned here) in the volume *L'uomo-dio* (Man-God) which, in my opinion, give a certain measure of Corsi's thought. It is focused toward the exploration of the primitive soul of the son of God: the universal emigrant, the poor man of the universe, the fugitive, the seeker of work or of illusions, the creator of myths and, at the same time, the prisoner of social rage, the *illuded,* the psychotic, the maltreated, the resigned, the sexualoid and the emasculated, the jokester, the loner.

Peons and Indians in the desolate Mexican lands, or waiters, prostitutes, wandering philosophers the love – sick and sorrow – tormented, either because of congenital inability to communicate or because of the opposite vice in the city ghettos are figure of the same human and hallucinated prism that Pietro Corsi, with a simple, almost memorialistic art, stirs to the infinite. A lowering of tone or a sudden lifting of wind, the chatter of the aboriginal markets and the suspected silence of the empty life never escapes him. Corsi measures with a clock-like accuracy the approach of a character and, with him, his darkness, his mystery.

The people who populate this yet unpublished book are figures, birds of passage, shadows burdened with absence, at times only voices in the petrified alley of thought: a main door squeaks, someone who is leaving, a festive gathering at twilight, the motionless and absent sky over nature.

And these people come and go, back and forth, at times recounted in the first person singular and at other times in the third, with the writer who observes from his distant corner, and on other times with the writer who mingles with the scene created by him: he talks with the character, draws parallels between his wandering life and that of his counterpart, the *indio*, the Indian, the man-god, that is *in-God*.

One of these stories of Mexican emigration that bears the title *Il miracolo*, under Pietro Corsi's pen, becomes an unconscious reactualization of the morbid Machiavellian jest of *La mandragola*. A man without offspring, deeply desiring to have at least one son, finds one day to be, finally, a happy father – on account that his lovely wife has been impregnated in the dark by a no-face, no-name, who used on the lady the mandrake.

And in the story of the Indian of Alvarado, the little street peddler who invents the song of the sirens, one finds the unconscious reactualization, in terms of fable, of the dreamers of the Apocalypse whom the Aztec emperor Montezuma, fearful of dreams, had violently killed in the presence of his assembled court. Carlos Fuentes comments that by having the dreamers killed Montezuma hoped to kill the future.

In Corsi's Indian, Montezuma's role is assumed by the policeman of Villahermosa who sees no meaning in the song of the sirens.

This fabulistic flow is tinged, finally, with a moralistic vein. For it is the intrinsic religious voice that winds, unseen but insistently intuited, through Corsi's novels. The bond with Carlo Coccioli, an Italian Catholic expatriated writer and in his way also a wandering emigrant, must have had a certain influence on the psychoromantic fantasy of the writer Corsi. With the positive realization, on our part, that Pietro does not propose messages or solution to life's sorrow.

It is to be noted that Corsi's style, always sober and gentle, invites to a reading without traumatic shocks. But at the same time it induces to curiosity, to a subtle sinfulness, to a participation with an exclamation and a question mark. In short: to reflection. And this is the intimate lesson of the nocturnal writer Pietro Corsi: Italian or Italo-American writer?

Of him we shall know more when the new dawn will have arrived.

Giose Rimanelli
Susquehanna Valley, July 1990

Printed and bound
in Boucherville, Quebec, Canada by
MARC VEILLEUX IMPRIMEUR INC.
in September, 2000